CHARACTERLESS
by Sundari Gibran

Characterless

Sundari Gibran

Published by Sundari Gibran, 2023.

This is a work of fiction. Similarities to real people, places, or events are entirely coincidental.

CHARACTERLESS

First edition. August 23, 2023.

Copyright © 2023 Sundari Gibran.

ISBN: 979-8223486145

Written by Sundari Gibran.

Also by Sundari Gibran

Pranayama: The Yoga Breath
Characterless

Dear reader
All the stories told in this novel are happening
in an Indian environment.
If you are not an Indian, you may have
difficulty understanding some things,
but you will understand the main story.
I hope you will enjoy it.

__N. B.:__ You cannot marry your first order aunt, but you can marry your second or next order aunt. That means you can't marry your father or mother's sister, but you can marry their cousin. And that relationship also exists between the two main characters in this story.

1.

Bobby, you are my soul. I'm willing to do whatever you say.

No, you're lying, Richie. What if I told you to do everything with me now?

Yes, I can. Tell me where to go? Let's go.

Then be ready. Not today, tomorrow evening we will go to the tea garden. Then, we will enjoy it very, very much.

Okay. But if I get pregnant?

Damn. Nothing will happen. I will make all the arrangements. Can I hurt you? You are my life.

Okay. If there is still some problem. Suppose someone saw us in this situation, then? It will be very infamous for me. Will you marry me?

What are you talking about? You are my wife. That's why I can't find happiness without spending time with you. You know, I'm going crazy. When will I get everything from you?

Tomorrow.

Oh, I can't anymore. See how it is now.

You're a savage.

I know that I am a savage. Say something else, something new?

Shut up? Mad one. Let's go now. My elder brother will come home today. If he doesn't see me at home, it will be defeated. Will scold terribly.

The two have been sitting by the dam and talking since that afternoon. Where two inexperienced young men and women are being flooded with sexual talk in the name of love.

Every day some villagers see these two are sitting. But no one dares to say anything. Because Bobby's father, Mr. Patrick, is a local assembly member and a rich man in this area. So no one dares to say anything to his characterless son.

In the evening, the two of them left. And Bobby came home, got a letter for him, opened the envelope and saw a letter from his married ex-girlfriend Neha.

BOBBY,

I am writing you a letter in great danger. Can you come to my home?

Now I am alone. Antony won't be here for the next four days. Come over. The rest will be later.

Your Neha

2.

Short letter. It's a sudden letter almost two years after Neha's marriage. Bobby's first love, Neha, got married two years ago, absolutely arrange marriage.

The next day, Bobby went to Neha, when Bobby was supposed to be with his current girlfriend, Richie.

There was no one except her.

Neha's husband, Antony, works in the police. Currently, his posting is in another city. But he comes two or three times a week.

Why do you suddenly write a letter after so many days?

Bobby, can you forgive me?

Why?

I left you.

I forgave you long ago. Now, why you call me again?

Why can't I call you? Have I done anything wrong?

Did I say that? But I want to know the reason for the sudden call?

I'll tell you everything. Be patient. You came from far away.

I don't have much patience. Tell me now. I'll be back today. I have a special job in the afternoon.

Did I become another one so soon? Why are you desperate to leave?

No, not at all. Yet you are someone's wife now.

And you? Have you become another one?

You can think whatever you want.

Bobby, I can't anymore. Shut up.

Then both of them became silent for a while. Neha went to cook.

What will you eat?

As you wish.

Then, I am bringing eggs and fried rice immediately. You get a little fresh.

At noon, even in this heat, Neha cooked and brought it in front of him. Bobby looks on in amazement, even though she has become someone's wife, but her loyalty and love for him have not vanished like camphor.

No matter what Bobby says, the reason for his arrival is the fascination with Neha's body. So Bobby, like the robot, sat down quietly to eat.

Let's eat together, Neha.

No, you eat first. Then I will. You are my guest.

No, I am not your guest. We will eat together. Otherwise, I don't eat alone.

Okay.

When Bobby wanted to return in the evening, Neha says, "You don't want to know why I called you?

Yes, tell me.

Bobby, don't you love me like you used to? Bobby doesn't answer.

Bobby, after I left, there was no one new in your life? Bobby is silent again.

Well, I understand. You don't want to tell me anything, do you?

Neha, what is the benefit of knowing all this? Now our road is very different.

Isn't that the answer to my question, Bobby? Tell me if anyone has come into your life?

Yes, I love someone else now.

Who?

She was a friend of both of us.

Richie?

Yes.

Bobby, have you changed so much? She used to exchange our letters.

I have not changed. Times have changed. And Richie is a very good girl. When you leave, if she doesn't... I told him, "Richie, please save me. Otherwise, I won't survive."

I understand. But why, Richie? She will be your aunt. She is your grandmother's own sister's daughter. In the end, you are with your aunt... What a disgust to think.

I have to go now, Neha. I have no more time. If I'm late, I won't get a car. It's already night.

Bobby, stay with me. You go tomorrow morning. Please.

No. I can't. Besides, if I had, people will call you characterless, and I don't want that.

I see your infatuation for me. Didn't you think of this notoriety when you ruined my body day after day before marriage? Bobby?

Then I thought you were mine. Now you are someone else.

No, Bobby, I'm still yours. Only yours. I can't forget the happiness of every moment spent with you, and I will never be able to do it. Can you give me back that day? Believe me. I couldn't be happier with Antony. Antony loves me very much, believes me, but I was yours, I am still yours, and I will be yours forever. How can I forget you, Bobby? Can you tell?

Bobby is silent. And he looks at Neha's beautiful face. But Bobby was supposed to be with Richie at this time today. He thought he would be back soon. He didn't tell that they would not go today on the famous banyan tree, north of the tea garden. Richie seems to have gone home frustrated while waiting. He won't even come to my house to look for me because people view our relationship with grave suspicion. Bobby became negligent to the thought in his mind.

Bobby, what are you thinking? Why are you silent?

Nothing.

Then why are you silent? You haven't said anything for a long time. Will you stay with me tonight? Please don't say no!

Yes. But I won't do anything.

You will get a very open opportunity. Think? You don't have to take any protection. Remember Bobby, it was a disappointed hope of yours for a long time, didn't it?

Bobby can't stay. Her body is numb, and he hugs Neha like crazy. They kissed each other and filled each other's chests. It was as if two hungry sex gods, who had been dissatisfied for a long time, were burnt to ashes by the fire of youth and jumped into the flame of sex. And the door closed.

RICHIE HAS BEEN SITTING on the edge of the dam for a long time. The mind is not accepting this. There is a pain in her mind. "Why didn't Bobby keep his word?" She comes back home, thinking. Returning home and serving the old bedbug mother. In the evening, she gave tea bread to her dad and younger brother Clifton. She is again wondering if the side of the dam will turn a little. Has Bobby come?

Avinash, "Richie?" Her father called to her.

Richie said, "Yes, Dad."

Finish cooking. I am not feeling well today and will eat early today and go to sleep. Where did Clifton go?

I don't know. Why you're asking me? What time does he stay at home?

At that time, one of their neighbours came with a request to write an application. Avinash sat on the outside balcony and wrote the application.

The neighbour is a young husband abandoned woman, Arupa. No one knows where her husband fled with his six-year-old son two years ago, leaving behind a baby girl to her. Now she spends her days making handicrafts. Sometimes Richie's father, Avinash, spends the night in her house secretly and gets various help in return. But Arupa addresses 60-year-old Avinash as 'Uncle.' It's not her own uncle, father's cousin.

Uncle, I lost my National ID card. How do I get a new card?

Don't worry. I am writing an application, take it, and submit it to the police station.

Why?

Suppose you don't give the diary to the police station. How will the authorities understand that you have lost your National ID card?

Police?

Don't be scared. I'll go with you. All right?

From the room, Richie's mother asked him who came out. Richie tells all.

And immediately, Richie's mother Nila got furious because she got the news of an illicit affair of Arupa with her husband from other neighbours long ago. Even though her body became paralyzed, her mouth wasn't closed.

She kept saying, "This prostitute is ruining my family. Richie, call your dad. Today I will worship him. He feels sorry for that prostitute. I will tell Francis everything. If I don't beat that prostitute by him, my name isn't Nila?"

3.

Bobby returned home after spending almost two days at Neha's house. When asked by his mother Kalpana, Bobby effortlessly covered up his notoriety, saying, "I had to go to town to a college friend's house to apply for a job test." And his uneducated mother believed that behind the affection for her son. Her mother is much more arrogant than ignorant. And the reason for her pride is that she has three young sons and her husband is a Member of Parliament. He has a betel nut garden spread over an area of one square kilometer about two hundred bighas of cropland, besides, her husband owns a Cane business. And the house is also the largest in the whole village. It isn't easy to find such a place even after visiting ten villages. They had a permanent shepherd, Naveen, to look after the cows, goats, and sheep in their house. He is a permanent servant of service round the clock.

At night Bobby, Robbie, Robert, three brothers, and their father, Mr Patrick, sit down to eat together. Kalpana Devi is feeding them, and Lesa, their permanent housemaid, is helping her.

While eating, Mr Patrick asked his second son, Bobby, "Where have you been for two days?"

Why? I told mom at noon, dad. Didn't mom tell you anything?

I heard. That was a lie. Now I want to listen to the truth from your mouth.

Bobby thinks. Did dad see him go to Neha's house? He is silent.

Tell me who sent the letter?

Which letter?

"Which letter" means? Stop acting, Bobby. It came in my hand first, and I read it and covered it again with glue. I have noticed all your incidents in these two days. I didn't hold you red-handed because I am giving you one last chance. I don't expect that from you.

At night Kalpana and Mr Patrick lay down and started talking about their sons.

Did you read his letter?

Yes. And what I saw from two days today!

What do you see? Where didn't say anything!

Your son has spent two days with Neha. I followed him from a distance by my employee. He doesn't know.

What are you talking about? But he said ... etc., etc.

Everyone says that. To cover their faults.

So?

See what happens? I'm worried about something worse than that. An illicit love affair with my aunt's daughter Richie has been going on for quite some time. I got a glimpse of the man's face, and I saw with my own eyes for two days, they sit by the embankment.

What did you see?

Bobby and Richie sit side-by-side on the tea garden's edge under the dam to talk.

What will people say?

Won't say, saying. People are saying nasty things, and I am losing my respect. Elections are coming soon. People will no longer vote. This time I got into a lot of trouble and became the father of such a character's sons. Your sons are ruining my money, property, nobility.

Bobby just made a mistake, so why are you slandering the other three boys?

If you hear what Robert has done, you will understand why I am saying this. Only he knows what he did with the girls in the name of love from class eight. But a few days ago, he and a few other drunks from his club hired a prostitute. In what they did all night, the girl somehow survived in the morning but is still very ill. She was admitted to the hospital by some people. See if she survives?

Defeat. What are you talking about? This is horrible news.

What else? Maybe she went to work for poverty, and they? Come and see what all of them have done to her.

Won't she die?

Maybe. However, I have sent money for treatment.

So? What will happen? What if she dies?

What if she dies? I have to pay the police to save your son from jail.

Well, sleep now. I will keep an eye on them from tomorrow. They both fell asleep.

CHARACTERLESS

A few days later, at about midnight, a man Entered secretly the house in front of Mr Patrick's. That is Arupa's house, and the person is her uncle Avinash (Richie's father Avinash).

Naveen gets frequent urination at night. So at night, he came to the side of the road and saw the story of the night. But he doesn't dare to tell anyone. But he was saying alone, "What he comes to do at night?" So when he could not resist his curiosity, he kept looking for a while. Going a little further, he suddenly said, "Who? Who's there?"

Immediately Avinash says, "I am, Avinash. Why are you here?"

Arupa immediately agreed to Avinash's words and said in a hoarse voice, "What are you doing? If you shout too much, I will slander your name. Keep your mouth shut and get out of here right now. And if you don't keep your mouth shut, I'll entrap you."

Arupa and Avinash chased Naveen away like a dog. And the shepherd, Naveen, also left. He stopped on the way. Seeing Robert, Mr Patrick's youngest son is entering the house late at night, but Naveen doesn't dare to ask him why to enter the house late at night. He is a servant, and Robert is Mr Patrick's, meaning Naveen's owner's son. So this time, too, Naveen kept his mouth shut.

However, Naveen knows very well that his owner Mr Patrick is not characterless anymore. He is a very good man. Yet, Naveen has a lot of doubts about his other three sons except his eldest son Robbie. But that's the only thing he has to keep his mouth shut.

Early in the morning the next day: There was a lawn in front of their house on the opposite side of the road. There was a pine tree, and Lesa's dead body was found hanging from a rope. Naveen started screaming in great fear. Hearing that, everyone woke up that morning. Everyone came running, seeing that horrible scene. Lesa's parents also came, and they broke down in tears. The police came and took away the body. Then no news is available. After a few days, the people of the area quickly forgot about Lesa's death.

Bobby's house had a large color TV. Since the afternoon, the two neighbours have been sitting in it to watch a TV series called "Any day now" in the evening. Arupa and Nayan. Because they are too poor to buy a TV. They both make handicrafts, they are both husbands abandoned, they have a daughter each, and so they have a friendship.

No one in this house likes to see TV in this room of outsiders. Usually, Bobby turns on the TV. Bobby's mother, Kalpana, doesn't say anything but gets angry at the thought that the house gets dirty. Mr Patrick sternly told her, "Don't rush when someone comes to watch TV. Let them see, the election is upcoming."

However, no one has turned on the TV yet. So they are waiting and making crafts. If they make a hundred pieces, they will earn fifty dollars and earn that money one day, then they will eat. However, their whispering is going on. Arupa began, "Why did Lesa die by hanging? Do you know?"

There are huge events. I can say. But won't tell anyone.

No. I won't tell anyone. But tell me in a low voice, the wall also has ears. Be very careful.

Nayan also began to whisper carefully, which no one can hear except Arupa.

Lesa came to my house late at night that day. He knocked on my door and said, "Aunty? Aunty? Open the door. I'll be with you tonight. I saw the Titanic movie, so dad bit me. I come to stay with you. Aunty e e e."

And I also got up and went to open the door and immediately heard that Robert and Sherman had grabbed her. Lesa shouts, "Aunty, save me, Aunty." What were they bothering? She was a virgin. They were like two crazy dogs. The screams and cries of the girl are still coming to my ears. I feel guilty when I think.

You didn't open the door?

Are you crazy? They were both drunk. They watch adult movies in the club every night and got hot. So what horrible, brutal torture this young girl had in both. Even on the lawn of my house, but I hadn't the power to do something.

You could go out and call people by shouting?

What are you saying? Who is awake at night to hear my screams? And they both warned me out loud, "Aunty, don't leave the house, or we'll rape your nine-year-old daughter right away, and you won't be left out either. We don't care about the eldest or youngest. I eat everything. "And we were awake but didn't make a sound. You know what?"

Defeat. Then you did well not to go out. Someone seems to have come. Shut up.

Both of them sat hesitantly.

Bobby comes in and says, "Will you watch TV, Aunty?"

Nayan said, "Yes, Bobby would turn on the TV a little."

Bobby turned on the TV and left the house. Because some people were shouting outside and coming towards their home. In their backyard, everyone came together. One called, "Mr Patrick, please get out of the house, Mr Patrick? There's an arbitrator. You have to go now."

Mr Patrick comes out and says, "What happened?"

Lots of facts. Will tell the whole incident on the way.

Bobby usually loves to be very tidy. Even today, he is going to meet Richie with a handsome look. Today is the day to fulfil that unfulfilled desire. So it's for that.

4.

Bobby likes to be a little tidy. His favourite dress was a white, ironed shirt and black pants. Also occasionally he wears wet pants and collared T-shirts. However, apart from his first love Neha and his second love Richie, no bad character record has been recorded yet. In that case, Bobby's younger brother Robert has gone on to do a PhD. However, there is enough friendship between the two.

Seeing Bobby's peacock-like outfit in the afternoon, younger brother Robert asked, "Are you dressing up a little more today, what's the matter?"

Nothing.

Tell me? I'm smarter than you, so stop saying this. What is the truth?

I know. I keep your news too. What about the girl you hired? Is she alive or dead?

She died a long time ago. Which we have cracked.

There was no case? Nothing happened to you.

Is there anyone to go to the police station and write a case for this prostitute that we have to go to jail? That's a trivial matter for the present age.

So you killed an aquatic life?

Who knew she would die? She was a virgin, so she couldn't take us. Here we haven't any fault.

You are so wrong, Robert, but you don't have any remorse.

And you? Are you shaking too much knowledge? You are in love with our aunt. What right thing have you done here? Richie is my father's cousin, how is your girlfriend? Tell me first, then I will regret it.

I don't think Richie is my aunt. I love her very much and she also. You won't comment on our love affair.

But people are condemning. So you fall in love with anyone other than her, we have no problem. Dad is angry with you. Do you know?

Will I fall in love with any other girl in one day or fall in love like a comet? How is that possible?

Can't do it in one day, love for days, months, and years, but leave Richie. And I have no value for this love. Is there anything called love? Do you chew it or rub it on the skin?

No. I see there is no point in arguing with you. But you have to be a little more careful, or you can be in danger. Got it?

You also manage. Exclude love with aunty. And when you can't argue, why do you?

Bobby left without further ado. But Robert's words seemed to ring in his ears. The term "aunty" about Richie made him feel very uneasy. But the representation is entirely accurate, so there is no way to protest.

RICHIE GAVE A LITTLE more makeup today than any other day. As soon as she left the house, her elder brother, Francis, called her back, "Where are you going?"

Let me take a walk.

Wait. I have a little talk with you.

What happened?

I chose one of my colleagues as a groom for you, understand? Very good boy, Anirban. The only son of the parents.

Richie stands silently.

Say something. I can't say anything to him without your opinion?

What else can I say? But I thought it would be better to get a job and then get married, right?

That's right. As far as I know him, he will accept your desire to work—very free-minded boy. I didn't tell you one thing.

What?

Without your permission, I showed him this picture of you that you took in a group with your college friends. You know what? He liked you very much. Once you say so, I can bring him to our house.

Would it be right to make such a big decision so soon?

All right. You think about a few days. I'll wait for your decision.

Without answering, Richie said, "let me go."

Hmmm. But come back before evening.

Okay.

Then she went out.

TEA GARDENS ON BOTH sides, the pitch road in the middle, has gone inside. On an autumn afternoon, a light wind is blowing, and a couple is walking. Sometimes there are big shade trees in the tea garden, and many birds are in it. It's like a beautiful eye-catching scene. The main road is above the dam. They walk through the sloping pocket road that comes out of that main road. Those who don't obey any relationship don't observe restraint, don't follow any prohibition. Today they are the flooded river, which at high speeds can uproot the giant stones of the mountains, the big trees. They love to be immersed in love, romance, lust, sexuality.

THE MEETING IS SITTING in the administrative officer's room. Local executive officer Ananta Barman, MP Patrick Chowdhury, Mrinal Master of the primary school are present. Emma is also present. She is present as the victim is an eighteen-year-old unmarried pregnant girl.

On the other hand, there is the unmarried Frederick present as Hunter. Although he is a cloth shopkeeper by profession, he looks around. This time he came to the right place and got stuck. Also present at the arbitration meeting are a few other dignitaries and family members of the victim and Hunter.

When Mr Ananta took charge as the chairman of the meeting, vice president Patrick Chowdhury started the arbitration meeting.

As vice-president of the meeting, Patrick first asked Emma, "Emma, will you answer some questions correctly? Tell me, what is the real reason behind your condition?"

"Uncle, it's not my fault. McIntosh said he loves me. Then our love lasted for about a year, and he told me many times that he will marry me in this one year. But now, he is lying under the pressure of his family. Now I have no choice but to die?" She cried.

Mr Patrick now asks Hunter Frederick, "Do you have anything to say?"

Yes. I did nothing. I never had a relationship with her. She wants to put her sins on me. And her mother and sister started quarrelling and supporting her.

On the other hand, when Emma's mother and two sisters started arguing with Frederick's family, Patrick raised his hand and repeatedly said, "Calm down. No one will display here. Our administrative officer, Mr Ananta, is the judge of this meeting. His decision is final. So there is no point in arguing."

Mrinal Master, an elderly and respected teacher, calmed them down by threatening them and left Mr Ananta in charge of justice.

The arbitration meeting is going on. On the other hand, Bobby and Richie have sweet sex by spreading paper in the tea garden's dry drains. Bobby and Richie are satisfied today. Fearing who would see them, they hurried to work and came out of the gorge again in a pocket road. It is a village, so there is no light post on the road's side so that everyone passing by can see it as clearly as daylight. And very few people travel on these pocket roads, so no one noticed. Their sweet moment didn't have to be captured in anyone's eyes, so there was no evidence. Again they are walking side by side, like husband and wife.

Richie asked Bobby, "Will you forget me after today?"

Why? Why this sudden question?

"And I'm not a virgin, it's all over. I'm so scared, Bobby. And my parents are pushing me too hard to get married." Richie described the afternoon incident.

Fear of what? I am with you and won't marry anyone but you. I promise. So don't worry, Richie.

But our family doesn't seem to accept this relationship at all. Moreover, society will look at us with hatred.

If they don't? We will go somewhere else and find our happiness. So don't worry about it.

Hmmm.

On the other hand, the arbitration meeting's decision was decided, and the responsibility of announcing the decision in public is given to Chief Mr Ananta.

5.

Based on the words of Emma and Frederick, the Hon'ble Administrative Officer of the Dharmanagar area conducted the trial. This is proved that Emma has been cheated on both physically and mentally by Frederick. So Frederick has to bear the responsibility of this condition of Emma. Or let the unmarried Frederick marry Emma. If he doesn't get married, he has to give Rs 25,000 as the fine. Cunning Frederick got rid of this problem by choosing the path of fine.

Emma fell into a big problem whose love and chastity was valued at only twenty-five thousand rupees. So they were forced to go home.

Although Richie and Emma aren't the same age, they talk like neighbours. Richie is anxious when he hears about Emma's story because Bobby won't do the same with her?

Unmarried mother Emma is now the hottest news in the whole area. Richie went to their home in the evening with his mother's permission. In front of everyone in their house, Richie asked Emma, "What will happen now?"

I don't understand anything. I couldn't even dream of such a big deception.

"What will you do now, Aunty?" Richie asked Emma's widowed mom Jamuna.

Will anyone marry with a child?

It seems that no one will agree to get married in this situation. However, by destroying the child, it will be comfortable with this twenty-five thousand rupees. What do you say, Aunty?

We think so. Let's see what happens.

One more week passed in these thoughts. Then they took Emma to Dr Chinmoy Dasgupta's private chamber. Richie had to go with them as a helper. Because they are uneducated, they need an educated person to talk to the Doctor, so they took her away with permission from her mother.

Richie told the Doctor all the facts about Emma. The Doctor then asked Emma, "When was your last period? Remember?"

I don't remember exactly. But in the last two or three months, my body has never been wrong.

Can you remember exactly?

No. I don't remember anything exactly.

Well, I'm writing ultrasonography. You will have to come back tomorrow with the report.

Two days later, they go to the Doctor's chamber with the report.

The Doctor said, "Look, according to the report, the baby has grown a lot. It's been about four months. And now it can't be washed anymore."

"Then what shall we do, Doctor?", Jamuna asked very worriedly.

The Doctor said, "There is little reason to worry. She will have to have a normal delivery by abortion. For that, the nursing home charge will cost around ten thousand rupees, and the patient will have to stay for four or five days."

Jamuna said, "Ten thousand?"

Hmmm.

Paltu, Emma's brother, said, "Okay, we agree."

Then admit him to the Merciful Nursing Home today. I am writing admission on prescription. Another thing is that there is a life risk for abortion, so you can think again.

Emma said, "I don't want to live, Doctor. I want to have an abortion anyway."

Jamuna heard her daughter say, "Nothing will happen to you. Don't worry. Everything will be fine."

Richie said, "Yeah, Emma, you don't have to worry. We're here."

Finally, they admitted her for the abortion, and everyone came out to come back. They had rented Nimai's jeep. They got up and sat down. Then two more ran and appeared there. They are none other than the two husbands-abandoned, their neighbours, Arupa and Nayan.

They came to town with their craft to take their owner's wages and now go home with the raw material from what they said. So they took the opportunity to go in their rented car without renting.

Nimai is driving his own car, and Paltu sat in the front seat next to him. There were eight seats at the back. Jamuna and Richie sat on one side. On the other side sat the two newcomers Arupa and Nayan.

At first, Arupa started, "The worst thing happened to your daughter. The little girl didn't understand. That's why she made such a big mistake."

"Yes, would it have happened if she understood?" Jamuna said.

"So. Now do abortion. Let her live, and you live too." Nayan said, getting a chance.

Frederick is the worst guy. I am getting old, my daughter is about ten years old, and he talked nonsense with me—a third-class guy.

Arupa, "What did he say to you?"

One day I went to her shop to buy a bra, then he asked what my size is? I said, give me one that will fit me.

That's right, he didn't say anything wrong.

Didn't you hear the real thing? Then tell me, "Let's go to town and watch a movie." What a dare?

He told me the same thing one day. Do you know how I am? I told him to get married and go to the cinema with his wife, and if he ever says such a thing, I will beat him with my shoes.

"Great, Great." Richie said.

Arupa said again, "And since then, she has been talking a little cautiously in front of me whenever she goes to buy clothes in her shop."

They came home talking, discussing, and criticizing.

BOBBY TOOK THE CANE business from his father, Patrick. Because if he won't be self-reliant, it won't be possible to get married to Richie. Patrick also wanted to retire this time. He arranged for the four sons to do business. For so long, Mr Patrick has been looking after his own cane business. Cane comes by truck from the Sundarbans, and some workers make mats and handicrafts by it. Then the product goes to the market at a higher price. And he earned a lot of money. Now he left it in Bobby's responsibility.

Bobby is not home for a few days on business. Richie has been told everything. Still, Richie is upset. Time doesn't pass. That was not the era of mobile phones. Some rich people in the village had landlines in their homes, such as Bobby had landlines in his house, but Richie's didn't.

In Bobby's absence, Richie was gone as Emma's assistant for two days to care for her at the nursing home. Last time, Jamuna took her with them with the permission of Richie's mother, Nila. And this time, Richie is here with the consent of both mom and dad.

Bobby sees the Sundarbans for the first time. Sundari, Garan, Gewa, Hetal, Golpato, Hogla, Cane, and many other plants. And what a beautiful view of the seashore, as if there is nothing else in life. But Bobby can't enjoy it because his love, Richie, is not here. That's why Bobby missed her so much. Bobby's truck driver Rakesh Gupta, although his mother tongue is Hindi, has also learned Bengali. It has been a long time since he left his native Bihar. Now a permanent resident of Bengal, he has been travelling by truck from Dharmanagar to the Sundarbans for a long time. Rakesh became excellent friends with Bobby.

Loading goods from the owner was done long ago. They had already packed some food from the hotel. The truck stops, and they sit on the side of the road behind the car to eat. It was accompanied by hand-made bread, chicken, and Rakesh's favourite drink, beer. Although Bobby has never been intoxicated. In which his younger brother Robert will get Star Marks. Robert is as characterless as a drinker. However, elder brother Robbie and Bobby have not been intoxicated yet.

Rakesh gave more meat to his current young owner Bobby. And after eating, Rakesh said, "Would you like some beer?" Although Rakesh is eighteen years older than Bobby, he is the son of his owner Patrick Chowdhury and the current owner, so he speaks with respect.

Bobby said, "I'm not intoxicated, Rakesh."

So what do you do in life? You did nothing. What taste! Ah, the world becomes new as if I am coming to visit heaven.

No. No. I don't drink Rakesh.

Eat a little. If you feel bad, I will never ask you to eat again. If you don't drink, how do you know what it tastes like?

Bobby drank for the first time in his life. Although it is for indomitable enthusiasm, curiosity, and Rakesh's provocative words.

6.

Bobby's truck driver Rakesh drank three bottles of beer and started driving. Excited, Bobby drank four glasses of water mixed beer.

Then Rakesh plays a song," Ka.... a ... a ... ta la..ga..a"...

Rakesh shook his head and sang to the beat of the song. But the intoxicated Bobby can no longer sit in the seat. His body was numbing, and he wanted to lie down.

Rakesh, I am feeling vomit. Too much...

Damn. Why vomit? I am not intoxicated. After crossing the Farakka, I will have a bottle of beer and drive with fun.

Rakesh... My body is getting confused,

Damn. Sit here quietly.

I can't sit. I want to lay...

Well, Lean your seat and lie down here. Try to sleep. Sleep will cut the intoxication.

I am feeling sick. What to do, Rakesh? Stop the car.

Why? What to do with stopping the car?

As soon as Rakesh stopped the car and approached Bobby, Bobby vomited on his body.

What an awful smell! Bread, meat, and wine combine to form an indigestible substance, just like hydrogen sulfide gas, which smells like rotten eggs.

Oh god, what did you do? You make the whole car dirty.

Rakesh started cleaning everything. Bobby is the owner of his livelihood. So he silently endured the stench of vomiting. He encouraged Bobby to drink beer, so he kept quiet because he deserved the punishment. He splashed water on Bobby's head, cleared his vomit, and changed his dress. He sat for a long time, and the wind blew with a palm leaf fan on Bobby's head. Bobby has become so weak.

Rakesh rubbed his nose and ears many times in his mind. He will Never let him drink beer again. His intoxication became useless. So he also drank a few glasses of beer and started his journey again.

Emma's abortion is at noon, so she has kept with saline since yesterday. The doctor stopped her eating rice, only saline, and injections. Richie was sitting next to her. Many more new patients appeared in that room. Everyone is pregnant. They came with their husband, parents, and many more relatives. They are overwhelmed with their love and affection. And they will return home with the child and a lot of joy.

Emma's stomach began to ache in the morning. She went to the bathroom a few times with Richie's help, but she didn't defecate. Her abdominal pain began to increase.

Emma moaned in unbearable stomach pain, just saying, "O my God ... Stomach is aching ..... I'm going to die of stomach ache...Richie ..... Save me... Richie, call the doctor ....mom, call the nurse. Oh, mom. "Talked a lot more.

When she started crying very loudly, a nurse came and carried her on a stretcher. And they took her to OT. Richie was sitting alone next to Emma's bed. After a while, her brother Paltu came, "Richie, Where is Emma?"

They took her to OT.

Oh.

They were looking for the Guardian. Go and meet them at the office.

Well, I am coming from the office. Mom is outside ... Will they let us come now?

I don't know. Visiting hours are from twelve. Will come after an hour. And what will she do?

Ok. We'll be back later.

On the next bed, a lady named Ruma was admitted. In unbearable labor pains, Ruma is just going to tell her mother-in-law, "I can't endure anymore. It's so painful."

"Be patient. Caesar will cost a lot of money. Thirty thousand rupees will be the bill." The lady is getting restless crying in labor pains, but her mother-in-law won't agree to Caesar at all. She wants to have a normal delivery.

I can't stay anymore. Tell the doctor to Caesar.

The mother-in-law is just saying, "Is it so easy being a mother? Endure a little more."

Finally, the mother-in-law agreed when the doctor came and said the baby was over-sized. Then she was taken to OT on a stretcher.

The woman's mother-in-law asked Richie about Emma. Richie told her everything.

Then she said, "Defeat, does anyone make such a mistake? The girl's life is destroyed."

"Yes, that's right." Though she said this in her mouth, Richie's body was almost curled up in fear, thinking of the tea garden's incident in her mind.

A few more came forward, very curious to hear this. What a shame. Why did she come to guard Emma?

"Who is she to you?" Ruma's mother-in-law asked.

"No one. Our neighbours." Now Richie has no desire to defile herself with her friend, relatives, or sisters' identities.

After the abortion, they put Emma back to bed. And some scavenger took the flesh of her stomach. Today dogs and cats will have dinner with it. Is this the result of love?

Emma's mother and brother all come to see her. "How are you?" Everyone asks.

"Good." In her mind, the joy of not being humiliated is greater than the grief of losing a child. So the current answer is "good".

Some people came again and asked her mother about her.

Meanwhile, Emma is suffering the grief of losing a child as a mother, cheating in the name of love. Her mother and brother have to be insulted. This condemnation, shame, humiliation, sorrow, hatred, criticism, where did you not remember the time of sweet sex? So this has to happen in Emma's life. On the other hand, Emma's lover, the cheater didn't get endless labour pains, didn't lose his honour because men's honour is not as cheap as women's honour. So Frederick now started looking for another foolish victim.

A week passed. Emma recovered and came home. But it would be better to go somewhere else than to hide. And everyone started trying to get her married. Even after such a significant incident, Emma's beauty didn't change so much, she is still an icon of unique beauty. So everyone thought it would not be too late to get married.

A few months passed. Richie finally got a simple job. Book proofreading and salary are only two thousand rupees. What if the pay is two thousand rupees? Once you see the competition that started to get the job.

At last, Richie got the job because of her Cousin Mr Patrick's recommendation. So Mr Patrick asked Richie to meet him privately at the regional office. Richie's father, Avinash, informed her.

Mr Patrick is Richie's brother, her cousin, on the other hand, he is the father of Bobby would-be father-in-law. So she is thinking a lot. What will address Mr Patrick now? Huge problem. Richie's mother Nila and Mr Patrick's mother, Anila, are sisters of one mother.

Mr Patrick was sitting alone in an empty room to tell Richie some secrets. As soon as Richie entered the room.

"Sit down." He showed the front chair with his fingers.

Richie sat down. Her chest is tipping. Although Mr Patrick is her brother, Richie never spoke to him. This is the first time.

I called you here because I have something to say to you.

All right. Tell me.

Do you know who recommended you to get the job?

I know. You did

Do you know why?

No.

I want something from you in return for the job.

Richie blushed in shame.

Don't be afraid. Who are you about me? Sister, my cousin.

Yes. Tell me what you want?

I want Bobby back. You move away from his life. I'm much older than you, but I'm telling you you're not going to have a relationship with Bobby.

Hearing this, Richie could not say anything.

You won't tarnish my honour. I have achieved that honour by working hard. For your mistake, it will be destroyed. And no one will be spared from this sin. So there is still time. You and Bobby accept their blood relationship.

Richie saw darkness. How is it possible to give up love?

After saying these words, he left the house. And in the chair, Richie sat with a numb body and mind.

CHARACTERLESS

Richie is in a dilemma. Love on the one hand and blood relationship on the other. Richie's life is full of tensions between the two.

7.

Richie joined the new job almost a month ago. It took a while to understand the new rules. Her office is five kilometers away from home. Her elder brother bought her a bicycle, which she used every morning to go out. Office time is from seven to ten, returning home at eleven o'clock. She meets Bobby on the way to the office every day. They met on the street beyond the familiar area of Dharmanagar. Bobby bought a new bike, with his own money, and an expensive mobile phone. Today he comes with mobile for Richie as a gift. So Richie was happy to see that, but said, "Why is this?"

I can talk to you at night. Do you know? I miss you so much at night, Richie. We will make love by whispering.

I know. I miss you too, Bobby. But my father wants to get me married. So I'm upset. My brother is also often looking for a groom. I got into a lot of trouble.

Let's escape, Richie.

Where to go? Here is your father's cane business and my job. What will happen if we go elsewhere? What to do? How do we eat? Who is sitting at work for us at this time?

I don't know. Won't go too far, Siliguri. I'll pick you up by bike in the morning, and leave by ten. Yet our dream of having a family will be fulfilled. You won't want to have a family?

I want to but you ... Bobby...you? What will you do? Will, your father, let you do the business?

Let's see if I can get a job. My father told me that if I married you, he would abandon me. Will also deprive of all property. So I don't think I will get the business anymore.

"As the son of such a rich family, will you marry me and work under someone else, Bobby? You have to give up all your relationships for the sake of your dignity and respect for me. You better marry someone else. Everything will be fine." Tears came to the corners of her eyes as she spoke.

And you? Can you leave me and marry someone else? There is nothing to do. Now we have gone so far, there is no time to think. You prepare mentally. We will leave Dharmanagar. How can we live where our love is not worth it?

"I didn't think so. But your happiness is my happiness." He looked at the sky and said, two drops of tear fell unknowingly.

Bobby's elder brother Robbie was taking the bike by the side. Sitting in the back is his girlfriend Jolie, the youngest daughter of Mrinal Master of the primary school. Jolie is currently in love with Patrick Chowdhury's eldest son Robbie. Jolie is lovely, in her first year of college. Her love record is very experienced. Her first love was with her current boyfriend, Robbie's younger brother Robert. It lasted for several years, then it was ruined. Then began another chapter. With Jolie's elder sister Pranati's brother-in-law Satyanarayana, people briefly tell the Satya. Then again with another sister Aroti's brother-in-law Arpan. Now everyone is discharged, and her last choice is Robbie. So people say about Jolie, "Has been in love with her younger brother for so long, and now she is in love with her elder brother, what a shameless girl!" But no one in front says. No one has the courage. Bobby and Richie stood on the bridge across the street, and their bike passed by.

EMMA BECAME VERY ILL after that incident. She could not cope with this shock. Day by day, her body began to break down, and after-abortion her body was already too weak. She is also heartbroken. Bleeding of her period didn't subside, yet she didn't tell anyone. The doctor told them to go again, but she didn't. Day after day, blood kept coming out of Emma's body. And in these few days, her body took the form of a formless eye-catching skeleton, a beauty less vampire.

The news reached the in-laws of Emma's two married sisters, and they didn't give it to them anymore. Her mother, Jamuna, repeatedly asked her daughter, "Emma, why is your body drying up?"

Nothing happened, mom.

Do you have a good body?

"Yes, mom." Lying entirely for two reasons. It will cost money to see the doctor again. She doesn't want to live anymore.

So that's what was to happen. Half of the twenty-five thousand rupees received from Frederick as the price of Emma's chastity went to the cost of the abortion. Twelve thousand rupees remained. But sick, weak, bloodless, characterless, stupid, ignorant, young girl Emma died in the end. Paltu bought a bike as a hobby for a long time with the remaining ten thousand rupees and fell in love with a young girl.

AT SEVEN O'CLOCK, JOLIE came to the street in front of their house and started shouting and cursing. Richie was going to the office by that road at that time. Stood up, "What happened Jolie?"

Don't say anymore. In the morning, I washed my red sweater and let it dry on the rope on the side of the road. Not here now. Which bastard took my sweater?

Oops. This? When did you?

This is ten minutes ago. In the meantime, which thief took my sweater?

It seems to have been stolen and fled. After a few days, you will be able to catch him when going out after your sweater.

If I can catch him, I will pee in his face.

Arupa is now going through this road. She stopped shouting and wanted to know. When he heard about the loss of the red sweater, she said, "Thieves in our area! Stealing things? Oh my God! I don't stay at home. I cook and eat and go out all day."

Don't leave anything out of your home.

I won't keep. Broom and my torn shoes have to be locked in and out of the home?

I don't know aunt! Where is your daughter then?

She goes to school. So this time I make handicrafts sitting in someone's house outside.

How much money can you make crafts?

I can't make more than a hundred a day.

When Richie saw that Jolie and Arupa had started talking, she came and passed by on her bicycle. And as soon as Richie left, the two of them began to chat again. Arupa said, "Do you know? Richie or Bobby is in love"?

You know what? I saw it with my own eyes. They are not ashamed to make fun of their own blood relationship.

Which bitch girl?

Yes, Aunty. Absolutely bitch girl.

But they kept analysing the character of Richie and Bobby by holding down all the pastimes they did. But Richie's first and last love is Bobby. Bobby's second love is Richie, and his first was Neha.

DECEMBER IS COMING to an end. The New Year is in front. The competition to build temporary cinema halls for showing videos has already started in the village school grounds. There is Robert's DVD shop, where the interest is very high. There are also his assistants.

Their cinema hall was made of bamboo and tents. Tickets to watch the film for only two rupees, there were a lot of sales. Pictures can be seen in a box more prominent than a TV. How fun it is to see the people of the village! And the cinema hall was in the city. The money to go so far, the affordability was not the people who worked in the village.

In the evening, Robert was sitting in front of his cinema hall. And a superhit movie is going on.

Robert said to his friend, assistant Paltu, "Paltu, let's have a good party tonight.

What's up? Got it. Who do you need?

You are saying that they are very cheap in the market! Rude one. Jolie has been in love with me for so long? But the bastard is now riding my elder Brother Robbie's bike. What can be done?

Boss, don't look that way. Terrible girl, very dangerous. There will be nothing if you force her to do something.

Did you just look beautiful?

Hmm, I hope she is dating with Robbie.

What to do? What do I do now? Tell me, Paltu. Give a good suggestion.

Let's take the car. There are more beautiful girls in the city than her. Just want money. If you have money, you will get everything!

No, the prostitute doesn't feel right anymore. You look for another option.

8.

There is a large betel nut garden on the west side of Mr Patrick's house. Early in the morning, his mother, Anila usually picked up the betel leaves and brought it. Then heated the water by them. His home has two wooden houses with four steps. However, the kitchen is enormous and made of bricks, cooking for the whole clan. After Lesa's death, Kalpana is now helped by another girl named Neomi. Neomi is the daughter of one of their poor relatives. Mr Patrick will be her uncle. Her mother and Mr Patrick's are cousins.

Now there is a storeroom next to the kitchen, where Mr Patrick stores grocery for the whole month. Besides, his eldest son Robbie has made wholesale of a grocery shop in the market, making his eldest self-reliant and happy.

Behind this kitchen is this famous betel tree garden to the west. There were also some jackfruit, different species of mango, lemon and guava trees in the garden. Anila is taking care of these. And in this garden is a place for children to play. Throughout the day, many games are organised.

Today Anila wakes up very early this morning and comes to the betel garden. But there are no betel leaves. Because Arupa and Nayan are very poor among the village people, they come to take the betel leaves, saying they will provide fuel. But on the other hand, the old woman lost her mood and was coming from the garden empty-handed, and the shepherd of the house, Naveen also got up very early in the morning and went to urinate in the garden, so he met her. Seeing Naveen, She came forward, "Have you seen betel leaves thief, Naveen?"

No, I didn't steal.

O fool, did I call you a thief? I said, do you see the thief?

No. Who?

Who will take it, I mean? Can't you see? Someone came and took all the leaves. I didn't get any.

Yes, I can see, but I don't see much in the distance. Did he take everything? So what happens now?

Yes, He's got to see now. Have you ever seen someone go this way? That's it. No. I just came.

"Oh my God? I wasted my time." She got furious and said, "Get away from the front."

Anila is in a horrible mood today. The betel leaves have been stolen for a few days, so she told his grandson Bobby about it at seven in the morning. Bobby, "Grandma, did you wake me up with so much screaming for it? I'll buy gas for you today."

Oh, my God! Are you my grandson or enemy? Do I understand anything about gas? I will die in the fire.

No. Grandma, you won't die. I will teach you everything.

Okay. I heard you did something wrong? Tell me exactly?

What do you want to hear, Grandma? So what is my relationship with Richie??

Yes, people are talking too much. Many have seen you talking on the side of the road. I'm dying of shame, Bobby.

Why the shame?

And what is your relation with Richie? Do you notice that?

Your sister's daughter is my aunt. But tell Grandma, what is the problem here?

There's no point in saying that, Bobby. I'll take action from your dad.

Do whatever you want, Grandma.

I will also tell Nila to notice her daughter.

You don't say anything to Richie's mother.

I will say. I will say it a hundred times.

Do whatever you want. I won't buy gas anymore.

I don't need gas. I'll pick up leaves. Still, you break up with Richie.

Bobby's grandmother Anil Devi and his mother Kalpana have no remarkable resemblance. But as soon as she saw her mother-in-law scolding Bobby for her illicit criminal love, she was pleased and joined her. Because the interests of them are the same here.

At noon Anila started her journey to her sister Nila's house. Not too far. She was walking along the road at the other end of the betel nut garden, and the little boys and girls of the neighbourhood saw her and all of them started shouting together. She got furious. So the boys and girls got more encouragement and started annoying her again and again. She called and grabbed them, hitting them with the stick in his hand but failed. Because how can an eighty-year-old woman with eight-year-old children? But where to go? Immediately she started abusing? Anila came out of the circle of these naughty children with great difficulty and came to her sister Nila's house. On the way, she met with her sister's husband, Avinash.

Avinash, "Are you all right?"

Yes, I'm fine, but I don't get any good news about you?

Why? What happened?

What is the relationship of Arupa with you?

Hey, she calls me uncle. Comes to ask for a little help. Nila must have said?

Yes, whatever she says, why? I'm telling you - the girl is not good. Stay away from her.

It will happen when you say so.

And what about your daughter Richie?

Excuse me, I, her mother and my eldest son try to convince her a lot, but she is silent. Won't answer anything. Now see if you can do anything? Ok, I go, I have a little work to do. Patrick called.

Ok.

The earthen house with a tin fence and tin canopy. However, with a bamboo fence around, nothing can be seen from outside the home. Anila came and entered the house. Richie came quickly and sat her down to get a chair. She and Richie's mother Nila meant a lot to her. But the result is zero.

Bobby went to Bihar with his truck driver Rakesh to buy business goods. They came with a plan to stay there for a few days. Bobby has learned a lot from Rakesh over the years. There was chalk in hand with beer. Now he has learned to drink wine, vodka and champagne. But Richie knows nothing. Bobby didn't drink any of this when he went to see her, and no one at home dared to drink for fear of Mr Patrick. Not even the world-drunk Robert. Then the two of them went from Bihar to Uttar Pradesh. Suddenly Rakesh said, "Bro, I don't want to drive a truck tonight anymore?"

Look, Rakesh, don't make fun. I can't drive a truck either, so you have to do it.

Ok, I'll. My whole body is aching after driving for two days straight. So what if we spent the night here and start tomorrow morning? I won't take any rest. I'll get you there in eighteen hours straight.

So you want to take a rest from the hotel? All right.

Yes, I have to take it. But there was a great thing here. I can see you if you want!

What thing?

A lovely bird.

Which bird is he?

Damn, isn't it just a bird? Lots of beautiful birds. Dancing, singing and caressing you a lot but the only condition is, it will cost money.

Shut up Rakesh. I don't want to caress any bird. You want to take a night rest at the hotel, but don't say these things in front of me. Besides, you know I'm engaged, and I'll marry Richie very soon.

Rakesh doesn't talk anymore. They then went to a hotel near the redlight area of Miraganj in Allahabad, Uttar Pradesh. The truck was parked on the nearby road. Rakesh has already said that he will stay in a separate room, and at night he will sleep only after working with a bird. So it is not possible to take one room. Bobby said nothing. However, the room numbers of them are sequential. At night Bobby sat on the hotel bed and ordered food and some alcoholic beverages. Then he called Richie. Talked until late at night. But there is no peace in anything, he keeps turning around and remembering Rakesh's beautiful bird's dance song. Sighing repeatedly. Rakesh seems to be dancing and singing with the birds for so long. Someone knocked on the door.

Who?

I am Rakesh. Open the door once.

Why? You go to your room and lie down.

Need a little, Bobby?

Comes out forced. Like he said, and where he has been for so long, a lot of money has arrived. Madam of that brothel has left his mobile phone as she could not meet it. Now if he doesn't give five hundred rupees in one hour, she won't give mobile anymore.

Oh Bobby, please come, get my mobile back. Tell me who is here except you now? And I don't have that much money.

"No. I won't go to this dirty place. I'm paying you. You go and get your mobile. I'll sleep now." With that, Bobby took out a five hundred rupees note from his pants pocket, slapped it on his face and closed the door. He thought to himself, "I can't do it anymore—this time I have to go home and play the secret game with Richie again. But if Richie disagrees? Let's see."

9.

Bobby came back home, met Richie with boundless interest, and offered to have sex in the tea garden. And immediately Richie snarled, "No. Never. I don't want to do anything wrong before marriage."

Why? Don't trust me anymore? Why change suddenly?

No. It's not a question of disbelief, Bobby, now I understand a lot. Don't be angry.

No. I will be angry. Will you meet there in the afternoon?

No. I can't.

You will meet. You have to.

No. I won't go anyway. It will be awful when people see it. Besides, I have a job now. I also have an honour. So you try to understand a little Bobby. Don't be so stupid.

No, I understand everything. You don't love me like you used to.

No. Bobby, you don't understand anything. Does love mean having sex? Tell, Bobby.

Bobby understands well, so he goes home without arguing. But Richie's refusal makes him angry. So he quietly drank some champagne and went to bed.

Have to go to Calcutta again tomorrow. A lot of work left. They will go by train because the goods have already been supplied by truck in Kolkata. Have to go to a meeting with some traders there. The train is at night. Teesta Express ticket, Bobby and his driver Rakesh.

Richie came to the side of the road in front of their house in the afternoon, leaving her wet hair to dry after bathing in the afternoon, after a suitable bangle as usual. How many people went to the market, saw Richie standing and watching?

Seeing Richie standing, Jolie stopped. After saying that, Jolie comes back to the main point. Jolie asked her directly, "Richie, do you really love Bobby?"

Yes, why?

Nothing. What else is love or that I will think about it? But I don't accept these loves, all are the same. So in life, you have to make wise decisions. And don't do any harm to yourself, Richie. Even though I am two years younger than you, I told you this, don't mind.

No, what else do I think? Everyone says the same thing, you don't say alone. What's about you? How is your love with Robbie?

Damn. He always searches an opportunity for sex.

What do you say? Seeing Robbie, don't think so.

What do you think? He is a complete hypocrite.

Well, is that so? When will you get married? If you don't, we can't.

We will. But there will be problems with your marriage. But I will help if any help is needed.

I need help, I don't know what will happen without you!

Richie, I have to go. The evening is over, I have to study. for the final exam as soon as the college opens.

All right, stay with Jolie.

Yes, I am. You don't worry.

They both went to their destination.

Today, Jolie's mind is bright having been able to talk openly with Richie. Jolie came home and saw Robbie already sitting in her room. Seeing Robbie sitting at home, she asked, "When did you come?"

This will be for ten minutes. Where did you go?

Why should I answer you from now on or go here and there?

No. I'm not saying that. I came and saw that you are not there. Your mom went to your elder sister's house.

What?

Just gone.

Why did you come here today?

Because of nothing, yesterday I proposed marriage to your father with my grandmother.

What? What did you say? What do we mean? What did you tell my father?

I like you, I want to get married.

You don't even need my permission.

Why Will I retake your permission? Your dad has agreed. And that's why they left with the opportunity to gossip about us.

"Shut up. Don't say another word. Who decides to fix my marriage without my permission? Robbie, go home now. I have an exam I'll study." Jolie kicked Robbie out of the house.

PARLIAMENTARY ELECTIONS are ahead, so a fierce battle has started between the political parties. Now there is no word on anyone's except election. Mrinal Master, Patrick Chowdhury, are the leaders of a group, so that they forgot their enmity and took an oath to work together, in a late-night school meeting. However, a young and quite energetic young man has appeared in this group. Name Jeet, Jeet Roy. A handsome, strong, six-foot-tall beautiful, thirty-year-old boy. His captivating use is such as to look looking. Giving political speeches is like playing. At present, this young man is a well-known youth leader. Their opponents are Mr Oni, a Congress leader.

The secret meeting ended with Jeet's speech, which was heard by hundreds of leftist people. "Let me tell you a few things in my very brief form. Why have we got our supportive government in the state for so many years? For our work. And if we want to continue our development work, we will win Mr Patrick by a vast margin. Let's take this oath and announce the end of today's meeting." And immediately, everyone agreed with him.

The night somehow ended for Bobby. Early in the morning, they left home. He boarded the train at one o'clock in the afternoon and then reached Sealdah station in the morning after finishing the night.

Now, the two of them reached the hotel to spend the night.

10.

Even after coming to Calcutta, Rakesh's naughty lustful nature didn't change. Rakesh went to spend the night with one of his slum girlfriends. And what will Bobby do? He cannot interfere with anyone's personal affairs. Even though Rakesh works under him, he still has sexual freedom.

Bobby took another room for him with so much money that it was difficult to adjust the room together. But as soon as he remembered a prostitute, he left the beautiful space and went to the slum to spend the night.

Bobby lay down with his blanket-wrapped. He didn't talk to Richie for two days. Don't say anything even today, he has fixed it in his mind. At midnight, the hotel manager comes. Knocks on the door. Bobby opens the door and says, "Yes."

I am the manager of this hotel. You saw me in the receptionist's room.

Yes, I saw you. Why now? I have already come with a roommate advance.

No. No. No problem. Do you need anything?

I have got everything I need. Now I don't need anything new. If I need anything tomorrow morning, I will call at 9 o'clock and ask for it.

You can tell if you want a drink.

Yes, I took the beer.

In fact, if you want to think of a girl here? I can give a little consideration for the first time. There are more offers if you become a regular customer, the rate will be much lower. You just say what age girl you want, you will get.

Bobby didn't want to listen but listened with fascination. Because the fire of Richie's rejection of sex is still burning in his mind. It's been two days, and he hasn't called Richie. He was so angry that he didn't receive Richie's call and didn't even answer any message.

Bobby sat down and said, "Yeah, send one of your own choosing."

And immediately the man gives a smile as if he had conquered a kingdom and left. And after a while, the door is knocked again. Standing in front of Bobby is a seventeen or eighteen-year-old girl. The girl came and lay down on

Bobby's bed and pulled the blanket over her body and said to Bobby, "Why are you standing there? Take off your clothes and lie down."

Bobby, the inexperienced boy of the village, stood beside the bed in astonishment at the shameless trunk of the girl and said, "Did you lie down?"

So what do I do? Madame sent me to sleep with you.

So, this way? I didn't see you well.

What to do? Will you marry me?

Bobby didn't answer. He turned around and said, "Still, if I want to have sex with you, I have to see if you like me."

How many girls of your choice have you slept with so far?

Bobby didn't have the answer either. So he said, "Get out of the blanket and sit here."

Well. As she was sitting, the beautiful 18-year-old Bengali prostitute sat down in front of Bobby, shaking her legs. What beautiful eyes, nose, face, not too fair but glamorous, attractive. And the silky hair of her head, the pair of eyes adorned with kajal, didn't look at her at a glance. The lips painted red with beautiful lipstick, uncovered pale neck, shapely breasts, slender arms, smooth fingers of hands, nail polish of beauty, nails in it, and wearing light jewelry of some imitation, unique as if an angel has come down from heaven. Bobby glanced at her and began to drink the flood of water of her beauty. Then the surprise broke. When the prostitute said, "How do you see? Do you like me? Will you marry me?"

Bobby can't answer, and she looks at him like a hypnotist. So the prostitute said again, "Look, there is no one else now. Everyone is engaged. I was not feeling well, so I was taking a little rest. But your hotel manager called madam and madam sent me."

What's your name?

One more thing. What to do with the name? I have come to be your companion tonight. Will I stay tomorrow or will you call me by name?

Yet I want to know your name, I have to call you by name tonight.

Call me by any name you like, I don't mind.

Yet you say your real name.

I am Pori.

That's your fake name!

No, that's my real name.

All right, go to bed, I'm coming.

ROBBIE WAS STUBBORN in Jolie's behavior and soon married him and took him as his wife and brought him to Sohagrat to crush all his pride.

That's why he proposed marriage to his father by his grandmother. But to no avail. Because now Mr Patrick is very busy with the election campaign, so his son's wedding is far away, there is no time to sit and cry even after his mother's death. The lure of elections and parties is nothing less than the interest of sex, alcohol and love. Mr Patrick has held the exclusive position of Member of Parliament for this Dharmanagar area for fifteen years. This position has become dearer to him than his father's property. He has ruled and threatened the people all his life. So now if he somehow loses this position, it will be more difficult for him than death. So now there is a strong campaign going on.

Richie, meanwhile, is upset. Bobby didn't talk to her until he went to Calcutta, didn't pick up the phone, and didn't even answer a message. Why did this happen? She doesn't think. Can people be so angry? Can he be so arrogant? After a while, she will be his wife and have a family for the rest of his life. Yet why not just endure these few days? Do all boys love the body of girls? Or love the mind? Richie can't think anything about all this. So she waited for him to come from Calcutta.

Mrinal Master's youngest daughter, Jolie, is now fully engaged in her studies. First exam, then love. Mrinal Master comes home after a party meeting in the evening, eating tea and talks to his daughter, "Jolie, they are talking about your marriage again and again."

Jolie knows all too well even then, "Who is 'they', Dad?"

That Mr Patrick's mother. Robbie liked you very much. So his grandmother asks me every day? What should I say? Tell me.

What else to say? I can't get married now. I will complete graduation first, do a job, then I will think.

Mrinalini, her mother, said a little at this time, "Yes, Jolie is right? But Robbie is a good boy. So how about holding them back for a while?"

Jolie agreed to her mother's offer. She answered her father's question, "you should tell the truth not to make something up. After my graduation, I am ready for this marriage."

Mrinal Mater, "Will they wait so long?"

Let's see. If they don't, nothing to do. I don't want to stop my studies by getting married in a hurry.

Meanwhile, Robbie has become restless to get close to Jolie. Because he has not had sex with any girl till date. But Jolie played the love game with him for a few days, but suddenly Jolie would say no like this in the marriage, Robbie couldn't even dream of that.

11.

Jolie's father, Mrinal Master, told Robbie's grandmother Anila about Jolie's decision to marry. These were all the discussions that day. Mrinal Master arranged it and said that after the graduation of Jolie they will marry her to Robbie. And if necessary, they can put the engagement, so that neither the boy nor the girl can go beyond this decision. Mr Patrick agreed, as his election would be over by then. And Robbie is happy for a while now because if the engagement is done then the way to roam freely in Jolie's house will be opened entirely. Can hope that one day it will be possible to drink the nectar of beautiful Jolie.

Jolie is standing on the street in the afternoon as usual. Robbie also goes to his shop in the market through that road. Seeing Jolie from a distance, the lamp of his sexuality lit up. A beautiful girl, with a bunch of hair hanging down to her back, and wearing a blue three-piece looks like a blue fairy. And why would Ravi Chowdhury be mad alone when sees her fair and beautiful face? It can awaken the sexual desire in the heart of any boy in the world. Robbie slowly approached Jolie at an average pace. He was furious for the previous incident, but still, Robbie stood up for a unique magnetic attraction on Jolie. Even though he tried, his legs didn't move. His legs became heavy enough to hold a vast rock, and he immediately stopped at the Jolie station with the brakes of his two running legs. Robbie suppressed his emotions as much as possible and asked Jolie very fluently, "How is your study going?"

Good.

Did you hear what my grandmother said to your father?

Yes.

"If we are engaged now and get married when you finish your studies, then you have no objection, Jolie?"

No. I have no objection. But if you expect more than that, I will have a strong objection, Robbie.

Does that mean more?

You know, it means more. So stop your acting, and I'm a very straightforward girl, so I like to say everything straight.

Got it.

Yes.

I have to go now.

Robbie could not go even after leaving. The mind is not obeying. Robbie came back again with a turn. "Jolie, I have something to tell you."

Yes, tell me quickly. My mom is not feeling well, the evening is coming, I have to go home early.

Hmmm, do you love me?

Yes. Anything else?

Hmm, if I give you a gift, will you take it?

After saying this, seeing Robbie's stupidity, she can no longer suppress her smile. Says, "Yes, I will. What will you give me?"

I haven't thought about it yet.

Well, think about it. I use nothing but branded things.

Then you tell me, what would you be happy to get?

How much money have you budgeted to make me happy? Then I will tell.

How much money, mean? Christmas is coming, so what if I buy you a sari?

Why not? I will definitely take it. But will you buy a sari? Do you know the name of any sari?

No. I will go to the store and find out.

Well. Let's see what you can bring for me. If it's right, it's perfect, and if it's terrible, you will suffer.

"Jolie ... Jolie e e e ..." her mom called from the room.

Jolie walked away without talking to Robbie, and as she left, she gritted her teeth and said with a charming smile, "Bye."

Robbie necessarily stepped towards the market.

BOBBY TASTED THE CUM off that eighteen-year-old beautiful prostitute all night and was filled with the juice of contentment. The night's fairy left in the morning and the manager came and appeared with a smile on his face. He said, "How did it feel?"

Good. How much do you have to pay now?

Not much. She was all night. So a total of two thousand rupees.

Bobby effortlessly pulled two thousand rupees out of his pocket. The manager was happy and took the money in his pocket and said, "What will you eat for breakfast?"

Now a little special liqueur tea and bread and jelly.

And what to eat at lunch? Will you stay today?

Yes, let's see.

Did you buy a ticket?

No. No. Tickets are bought.

Even if it is cancelled, there will be no problem. We will confirm tickets for you online, no problem. We have all the arrangements here. You can call us all-rounders.

Well. I found out when I thought about it. I'll take a rest.

Yes, yes. Take a rest. The whole night was no less disturbing!

Even though it was true, Bobby was ashamed to think of the reason. Because he has not yet signed up for such a shameless, characterless group.

But from today, his name has been included in the list of characterless people, so the manager dared to talk to him so much. So there was no way to protest. And he was really getting sleepy as a result of waking up all night. He said to the manager, "Yes. We will go tomorrow. You order a ticket. You have my ID card."

Very good. Sleep. Tell me what to eat for lunch, call once. No problem.

Yes, please go now.

When breakfast arrived two hours later, drank a whole bottle of water like a monster on a hungry stomach and fell asleep again. He got up at twelve o'clock in the afternoon when he heard the knock on the door. Rakesh came and sat in his room. Although Rakesh didn't know what happened to Bobby last night, he said, "Bobby when we will go? We have train tickets for the night."

Yes, there is. Rakesh, my body is not much better today, so I am thinking of going tomorrow.

What's funny is that there is no way to explain how happy Rakesh is with these words. If he could, he danced naked here. Because his beloved didn't want to let him go, now if he stays one night longer that's great.

In the afternoon, the two ate chicken rice, mutton, sour yoghurt and pulses, vegetables as they were. Not necessarily, they checked out Rakesh's room, and Rakesh went back to his slum darling.

MR ONI OF THE CONGRESS has a big problem with Jeet. If Jeet says the house will get free for the public vote, Anil says the toilet is free. Jeet says water is open and Anil says electricity is free. Jeet says ration is free, Anil says the bus is free, the truck is free, clothes, shoes, and underwear are all free. Free, free, seeing so much free stock, the general public went crazy. So once they jump to Anil's team, they jump again to Jeet's section. Now, the two parties' leaders also started pulling the public in their own party, and excellent tension started.

12.

Not for a day, not for two days, Bobby returned home from the hotel spending nights with many prostitutes for a whole week. He has returned home because he has run out of money. Otherwise, he would not know how long he would stay — ruined his character. But no one in Dharmanagar knew this, so everyone thought of him as before. Meanwhile, Richie just silently shed tears, with the sadness of not talking to Bobby, the despair of not being seen, the gloom of not making love. Bobby met Richie again and said, "How are you, Richie?"

As you left.

What do you want to mean?

You know very well. Why haven't you talked to me for so long? Or don't want to have a relationship?

No. No. Why not keep the relationship? So I was swamped. You don't mind.

You were so busy that once you didn't need to answer my call, once you didn't call me in person, just didn't answer a message. Why were you so busy that you didn't even have time to remember me?

Yes, I was swamped. New business, you know, how many meetings.

Did you have a twenty-four-hour meeting, Bobby? Is that what I have to believe? So just a minute, not a second. All you could do was call me and tell me you're busy. Then I would not have suffered so much.

Many prostitutes came to Bobby's room, again and again, hour after hour. So he didn't call so that the mask of this characterless would not go to Richie. So today, Bobby is busy proving his innocence by resorting to constant lying to cover up his guilt. The woman's ignorant lover thought that the lie was true. And Richie cried with his head on Bobby's chest in great pride, and Bobby's white shirt was soaked with tears. The tears in Richie's eyes left a black mark on Bobby's shirt. Bobby was deeply saddened by this, but he didn't have the courage or morale to reveal his sinful story's truth. That is why he stood deaf and dumb in the famous banyan tree by the side of the dam. In the distance, the beautiful red sun is setting. Birds have begun to return to the big trees in the tea garden, what a lovely garden with the sound of chirping. There are no other people around except these two. One of them is a worshiper of true love, and the other is a worshiper of lust. Bobby said, "Don't cry anymore. I'll call you no matter how busy I'm from now on. It's getting late. Go home. People will call us bad when they see you."

Let people say badly. I love you, Bobby.

Tears came to Bobby's eyes, the fire of remorse burning in his mind for ignoring this love. So he could not bear it anymore. Now he was busy trying to escape.

Bobby's elder brother Robbie is now too busy to please Jolie. He came to the market and decided to buy a perfect sari for Jolie. Such thoughts work. The largest clothing store in the market is Frederick's. This is the lustful person whose contribution Emma is no more in the world today. Whatever the character of Frederick, as a shopkeeper, he was sweet-spoken. His shop has all kinds of clothes, so there is no customer shortage even after a significant incident. Besides, cheap, expensive, brand all sorts of things are in his shop. The rich and the poor, all are satisfied to buy from his shop. And besides, why such a significant incident? How long do people forget? Frederick was very happy to see Robbie coming to the shop and said, "Sit Robbie. Tell me what you want?"

"Yes." Robbie sat down like a handsome gentleman.

What do you need?

A good sari.

For whom? I mean, if I don't know for whom, how can I understand?

For a girl of nineteen or twenty years.

"Oh. Well." He smiled a little and said, "Shall you take it for Jolie?"

It is difficult to deny the truth when it is said. So he was forced to say, "Yes."

"Good. Good. Now I am giving you a gorgeous sari. Wait." Frederick said and took out a lot of sari from the shelf. Said, "Look which one you like? This is Jamdani, this is Dhakai Benarsi, and this is the famous Rajshahi saree of Bangladesh, look which one you like? You see the design, I will show you a collection of different colours."

Robbie came to buy a sari for the first time in his life. No experience, now all the sarees look beautiful to him. And he is thinking a little. Suddenly he said, "Frederick, you give me this red sari."

Take this Jamdani. Tell her to wear it at Christmas, she will like it very much.

Robbie was embarrassed. He said, "How much is the price?"

"Don't worry about the price. I'll take less from you." He packed the beautiful sari and put it in Robbie's hand.

Frederick, how much?

Now I can't remember. I'll tell you tomorrow. Come once tomorrow. And say, what did Jolie say when she saw your sari?

Well. I will come. He took the sari packet and went to his shop again, but he can't wait to see how Jolie looks by wearing this saree. Today, the mind is no longer in the shop, even though there are two employees in the shop to deliver the goods, there is no work other than just sitting and counting the cash, but the crazy mind has become more stupid crazy? It was OKOK to sit in the shop like a vagabond until eight o'clock at night with great difficulty, but he couldn't do it anymore. So he hurriedly closed the shop, and dismissed the two employees and left for Jolie's house in a cowardly mood.

Seeing him, Jolie's mom Mrinalini Devi let him sit in the room with a very polite demeanour. Mrinal Master was also present at the house today. Robbie is the son of a neighbour, so Mrinal Master didn't show any particular formality and asked him directly, "Do you like Jolie? Do you want to marry her?"

Yes, uncle.

Well. Very good, we have no objection. But let Jolie graduate then.

Yes. All right. I'll wait.

Mrinalini sat by the bed, and Robbie sat on the sofa. Jolie came from the next room and sat on the bed next to her mom. And until now Mrinal Master was watching the news on TV, he said these things by turning off the TV when Robbie arrived, then a phone call came. Then, "Speak up. I'm coming a little. There's a meeting today too. Look, your father, Mr Patrick's call." He went out with the phone.

Mrinalini said to Robbie, "How is your business going?"

Very good. One thing, I brought a sari for Jolie.

Robbie sat shamelessly in front of his future mother-in-law and handed the packet of the sari to Jolie. Her mother was a little embarrassed and hesitant to see this scene of the future son-in-law's brazenness. But she said, "What is the point of all this?"

No. I thought Christmas was coming, so I gave it as a gift..

"All right." The mother-in-law left the house and went to the kitchen, saying, "There is some work to be done."

Jolie and Robbie are both sitting in the room now. One is sitting on the bed, waving his legs, the other is sitting on the sofa like a pumpkin. As soon as Jolie's mother left, she got angry and said, "Aren't you crazy?"

Why? What did I do?

What do you mean? Rude one, do you have to give this sari in front of my mother? Mad one.

Why are you talking so much? I didn't understand, and I thought you wouldn't be able to say "no" in front of your mother.

"Yeah, I can't say 'no'?" "You think you're brilliant, don't you? You have nothing in your head?"

Won't you open the sari?

Definitely will see but at my time. One more thing, what you have given now, you have provided, you will never bring anything for me again. And in fact, I won't accept, I said in advance, so don't make this mistake.

Why? Why not?

Because to be straightforward, I love to stay away from a giving-and-take-policy.

IT SEEMS TO BE AT TEN o'clock at night. There is not much time left before the election, Mr Patrick and Jeet are anxious. So a secret meeting is going on, and a few leaders are present in their party office. Avinash said, "It is difficult to win this time."

"I think so too." Mrinal Master said, "Moreover, the TMC will cut some votes, and BJP and independents will also cut some. For the rest of the voters, it is not yet clear how the election will outcome."

Mr Patrick said: "I've done a pretty good job of serving the public over the last fifteen years. My addiction to position and honour is more than greed for money. You all know that. But Mr Oni is ruining everything. Last time, those who were in poverty during the floods were given rice, pulses and tents with their own money. Did I know then that he was preparing to fight in this election?

Jeet Roy: I also can't think of what an advance plan! For the last two years, he has been selflessly benefiting people. Why not? His father has a lot of money. Donated one or two rupees for this day. Today it's proved. The clever man has already bought the votes of the people. No matter how much we want to convince the people that we will build a people-friendly government, people cannot say in front of them but are looking at it with suspicion in their minds.

Mr Patrick: Jeet, I told you to survey. Did you?

Jeet: I did. We will get forty per cent of the total number of voters here, but the rest is unclear.

Patrick: It becomes a problem. However, there is no other way but to continue giving charity. Pour alcohol on young boys, help those who lack money with some money.

Jeet: No worries. I'm trying, let's see what happens? Now everything is a matter of fate. But I will tell you one thing, uncle. You've spent a lot of money, so spend it with a little restraint this time. If by chance, something wrong happens then it will be deplorable.

Mr Patrick didn't answer. The meeting ended late at night.

AT NIGHT ROBBIE CALLED Jolie again, "Hello."

Yes, tell me?

Did you see the sari?

Yes.

13.

"Yeah. Very nice," Jolie said.

"Then I made you happy, did I?" Robbie said on the other end of the mobile.

Yes. You can, but there is nothing to be so happy about.

Why? Why not be happy?

If you think you can convince me for sex with a sari, you are very wrong, Robbie!

Robbie really got in trouble after hearing such an answer. But no matter how hard it is, it won't go away. So Robbie said fluently, "No. I don't think so, Jolie. But I always have a question in my mind, what kind of nonsense do people say about you? I don't know the truth about it, so I'm asking you directly. Why do people say this? Do you have the answer, Jolie?"

Hmmm, of course. When no one can fulfil my hobby of enjoying, then they make these stories. I've fallen in love with a lot of people, even your brother Robert. I am telling you: your brother is the number one characterless. When he couldn't have sex with me in his bed, he breaks up. And there are so many on this list, not just your brother alone. Two days later, I noticed the true nature of all those who came to enjoy my body in the guise of my boyfriend. Suddenly love is lost. And then they make up all sorts of weird stories about me that they had sex with me. But I didn't go to protest. I am silent because I am a girl, Robbie. How much power do I have to fight against this lie? Do you know?

Today I got to know you anew, Jolie. I'm really blessed to have you today. I love you, Jolie. Sleep, get up tomorrow morning and sit down to read again. It is not right to stay up late. Don't worry anymore. I love you with all my heart. Your love is too much for me.

I love you too. Good night.

Okay. Good night. Have a sweet dream. Bye

Robbie went to the Frederick shop the next afternoon to pay for the sari. He went and said, "Tell me the price, Frederick? You said that, will you tell me today?"

Sit down here, Robbie.

Robbie sat down.

You don't have to pay for that sari anymore.

How is it? Why not pay the price?

Yes, there are reasons.

Tell me why you don't want to take the price?

It's a big story, want to listen?

Yes, I sat down to listen. Tell me.

You know Emma is dead, I can say it's for me. You know I loved her from the bottom of my heart. I chose this sari for her. But it all happened so quickly that protecting my mom, dad, and relatives' honour became a big question. I got into a lot of crises, I ... yes I did it like a robot. Do you know, Robbie? I have done very wrong with her. I have cheated with the simple, innocent love, I have played with a girl's honour without understanding. Now every night I have nightmares, I get scared. Emma seems to be saying to me, "Frederick, could you do this to me? You could hurt me so much? Don't you love me?" I have no answer. Now she is no longer alive. It's too late, tell me where to go, to whom should I go? You think I'm a naughty lustful drunk man. You're right. I am so. I'm really so, but you know I have a heart. Who would I tell? Who will believe me? No one, No one will believe. And I gave this sari to your love so that your relation is deeper. Be happy when you get married. Don't make mistakes like me. Everyone can be fooled, but one's mind can never be deceived.

Robbie clearly saw a drop of water in Frederick's eyes. "Ok, ok. Frederick, forget everything. You'll see everything will be fine."

If you want to forget, can you forget? Is it so easy to forget? What can I say that the smiling face of Emma is like cutting my heart every day? The girl was insulted for me, I could not protest. She went to the hospital to ruin our baby, I couldn't do anything that day, I couldn't say, "This is our baby, this is the result of our love. We will be happy with it." I got the news the day she died. My eyes were watering that day, I couldn't stand to see the last one. I am a coward, heartless, lustful, and drunk. Emma really loved me. So I know she has forgiven me even though she is dead. But I can't pardon myself.

Frederick, can I say something? Get married this time, the new wife will actually start all over again.

No, I will never marry again.

A customer came to Frederick's shop, so Robbie left without talking.

JEET AND ROBERT ARE the same age, so they were sitting and talking. Jeet, "You know, my only hobby is to be king. I will have a lot of power.

Is it so easy to be king?

I'll be one day, you see.

How? What was the formula for becoming a king? Then I will try, I will keep a thousand queens. A. What fun! Tastes new every day.

What a hobby? Cope with greed, or you'll drown, and the formula for becoming a king is nothing. Going forward with politics. All-day long you can't see anything except the girl's body.

Are all those who do politics the king? You're telling weird stories. And if I don't become the head of this area one day, you name the dog after me.

But remember. Who dies? And who is the king?

At that moment, some people and a crying girl and her mother came in front of them, to the young leader Jeet for the trial of an incident that damaged a girl's modesty. Because the leaders are so busy with the election, the young leader has judged this rural incident.

14.

Jeet was suddenly shocked in the face of such a situation. "What happened?" Nisha said, "Mr Jeet, I was studying at my house this evening. My mom went to the house next door, and my dad went to the shop. There was no one in our home. Suddenly the electricity went out, so I sat down to light the torch. Mithun forcibly entered and made an inadequate offer to me. I shouted in fear and called out to everyone. When he saw everyone coming from the house nearby, he ran away. Today again and Mithun has been harassing me on the road for a few days now. And now I see that it is becoming difficult for me to get out because of fear.

Understood, tell me a little clearer, how did he annoy you? Then I see him. I will make mincemeat out of him.

Everyone stood quietly and listened intently to these conversations because they had just come to see the fun. Then again, such an exciting incident. Ah! Listening to these in one's own ears, watching real drama in front of one's eyes is different. However, Nisha's friend Divya spoke on his behalf, "Yes, Mr Jeet, she is right. When our school was open, he would stand on the street, Nisha usually is very scared to see him from a distance."

Well, why didn't you say this before? Where can I find him now? Will he stay at home after this shoot?

Nisha's mother said, "Doesn't it mean to be at home? He is such a shameless devil. Who knows what he will do when he grows up. He is at home. We have told his parents that they are rich people and have no problem with their son's behaviour. It's like showing kindness. But when it comes to playing with our daughter's dignity, we won't give up. There's a thing called society, isn't there? We want justice. We've told Mr Patrick, too.

Seeing the situation hot, Robert has fled so far so that none of his misdeeds is exposed.

Divya gestured to Nisha and said, "Tell those incidents, Nisha."

And at Divya's hint, Nisha started saying again, "Jeet, Mithun sometimes in my room, that is, in the room where I live, if I open the window of that room, he throws all sorts of dirty pictures through the window. One day I saw him with my own eyes throwing messy packets through the window. I don't dare to keep the window open anymore for fear of it. I keep the window closed all the time. I didn't even tell my parents about it, I just told Divya and showed it. And now if it is not appropriately treated, it will become like a tumour. It doesn't take long for a tumour to turn into cancer. It can lead to death. "

So Jeet said goodbye with the assurance that he would take the immediate step of action.

They too left with the feeling that the kingdom had really won, relying on victory.

Jeet and his team all went to Mithun's house and started shouting. Everyone in their home came out. Her parents are far-sighted and resourceful. And they have become masters at handling situations. Because there has been a lot of harassment for their characterless lustful drunken son before.

Jeet and his team were taken home like their son-in-law, while his parents won half the battle with tea, biscuits, cigarettes, sweets and remorse. So for the time being, Mithun survived from the slaughter. However, while leaving, Jeet went to Mithun's room alone and said something.

"Mithun, I apologized to you for making a mistake by looking at your parents' honour. But if you go to play snatching with Nisha's praise recognised or her parents' praise again, I will separate your bones and feed the dogs. I gave you this last warning. Be careful, and don't try to forget my words. "

"Yes." But Mithun became more vengeful in his mind. Nisha told everyone these things, in Mithun's eyes, she was a huge enemy and a criminal. But the beginning of this crime was caused by Mithun himself.

15.

The vengeful Mithun began making tactics to harass Nisha, and his assistant, mentor and only friend Ananta, Lesa's brother Ananta. Mithun and Ananta are of the same age, and they stay together all day at work. Mithun's father, Sundarlal Sarkar, bought him a truck. Because when he was not studying, he made this decision thinking about the future of the boy who got TC after failing in class eight several times. However, the driver of Mithun's truck was Ananta. The two of them used to go to different places. Although the two's nature and character are friendly to be the same, Ananta is a little above everything in Mithun.

Lesa, a working girl at Bobby's house, was raped by Robert and his friend Sherman in the middle of the night, on the lawn of Nayan's house abandoned by the husband. Then the police didn't file the case. Good, virtuous man and compassionate public representative Mr Patrick lost to his affection. So Mr Patrick knowingly covered his son's notoriety with money. And later, Lesa's impoverished parents became silent even after knowing and understanding everything because this is how the poor are judged. That Lesa's brother is this Ananta. The only younger brother of the raped Lesa is now a friend of the now-defunct teenage boy Mithun on the one hand and his paid employee on the other. Mithun and Ananta continue to plan.

Bobby felt remorse for what he had done, but now he felt comforted, thinking there was nothing he could do. He started trying to gain self-satisfaction. And Bobby thought to himself that he would never spend the night with these prostitutes again. Let's see, can Bobby keep his word? On the one hand, the sexual appetite of his own body, on the other hand, the self-loathing of cheating with Richie's faith, both of them are continually burning him. And on the other side of Bobby's bed is another single bed, in which his younger brother Robert is now snoring as if he had no worries, no thoughts, and no guilt. Happy and peaceful people like him can snore and sleep at all times.

Suddenly Bobby's mobile rang, an unknown number appeared on the screen, "Hello... who's saying?" Said very softly so that Robert would not wake up. Because this is where he falls in love with Richie in a shallow voice, and Robert incessantly falls asleep. He doesn't know all this, but he guesses a little bit.

A woman's sweet voice from the other side said, "Well, is this Bobby Chowdhury's contact number?"

Bobby's heart leapt when he heard the name of an unknown woman on the phone so late at night, and as surprised as he was, there was no way to deny it, so he said, "Yes, I'm Bobby Chowdhury. Who are you?"

Bobby stop ... stop ... I ... I'm Neha.

In just these two words, Neha's familiar voice to Bobby so far, the way she spoke, proved that this is Neha, His ex-girlfriend Neha. Bobby said, "Where did you get my contact number? I just bought a mobile. I haven't seen you in the meantime."

It's a big story. You can say I wanted it from the heart, so God gave me your number.

You're talking weird. Where exactly did you get?

Not weird, Bobby. It's a Miracle. We have had a great miracle.

Who gave you my contact number?

If you insist on something, you won't give up. You are stubborn. I don't see your stubbornness changing at all.

Would you say that? Tell me? If not, I won't talk to you anymore.

Bobby Wait, why are you running away in anger? I'm talking. Yesterday your truck driver Rakesh came near to our house to deliver the goods. I met him. I also stood on the street in front of our house, and Rakesh was walking, then we recognised the two of us. That's it. I asked about you. I heard your body is not right, so you didn't come? What happened to you?

Nothing. A few days ago, I came from Kolkata. There was a lot of stress on the body, so I didn't go to Siliguri. Tell me then?

Meanwhile, Richie's call is coming to Bobby's phone so many nights. But Richie got Bobby's phone is always busy. Richie is on fire with anger. Why is Bobby's phone busy so late at night? Who is he talking? Is Bobby cheating? Her heart was pounding at the thought.

In response to Bobby's words, Neha said, "Then I took your contact number from Rakesh."

Oh well, got it. But from whose phone did you call? As far as I know, you don't have a mobile, and it's not even a landline number.

Yes, this is not our landline number. It's my mobile, and my husband bought it.

Excellent. Why your husband suddenly bought a mobile?

Because I was stubborn, and there's good news, I'm going to be a mother. For you, the one you came for. I haven't had a period since then.

Your husband didn't understand that it is not his child?

Damn, how will he know? I have not been able to be a mother for so long because he has a problem. So I called you by letter then, you don't understand why I called you by letter. I kept it for two days by force. Ah! Bobby, what did you give? Fill me up—happiness, peace, with children. My husband doesn't know any of this. He thinks it's her child, so he's too happy. You know he stays at home for two days, so he bought this mobile to get my news.

So many shoots have happened?

Yes, a lot. Finally, our love succeeded.

Hmmm.

What does that look like? Thank you so much, Bobby, for being the father of my child. I will go crazy with joy.

You are already crazy, how can you be mad again??

Yeah, I'm crazy, Bobby. Fantastic for your love. You were my first and last love. Today my husband went to Dinajpur, and today I called you to give you so much good news.

Meanwhile, Richie keeps calling Bobby, and busy keeps showing up. Though Bobby talks to Neha, he also sees Richie's call. On the one hand, the ex-girlfriend is now overjoyed to be the mother of his child and on the other hand, Richie, the current girlfriend who loves him dearly, confidently believes. Where to go? This is what happens when you step on two boats. After this terrible love crisis, Bobby feeling hot even in the cold of January. Robert is moving a little on the other side of the bed. Bobby thought, what if he gets up? Then talking on the phone so late at night will definitely look bad. So Bobby said to Neha, "I'll talk to you about this tomorrow Neha. Robert seems to be getting up. Now you go to sleep."

Well. OKOK, you can't save my number by writing my name,

Why?

Richie will leave you to go if she finds my name on your contact list. And I don't want anyone to know about our relationship, especially my husband, Antony.

Well, I understood. Good night.

Good night

As soon as Neha's call was cut off, Richie's call and Bobby was forced to receive, "Hello. What happened?"

Bobby, who have you been talking to for so long tonight? Why was your phone saying busy? I've called you at least a thousand times. Didn't you see? Or don't you want to see? Tell me, what do you have to say this time?

Robert had been lying on the other side of the bed for a long time. He woke up, sat up, and went to the bathroom. He sat down and said to Bobby," who are you talking to so late at night? With Richie? I know. Now go to bed, it's three o'clock at night, and in two hours it will be morning." Even after saying these words, he opened the door and went to the bathroom. Bobby didn't answer Robert's words. And on the edge of the mobile line, Richie could clearly hear the words of her future brother-in-law Robert in her ear and could not bear it. She said, "Tell me, Bobby? Tell me who it was. Who did you talk to on the phone for so long that you didn't feel the need to answer my call?"

Richie, I will call you tomorrow morning and tell you everything. Don't worry unnecessarily. I'll call you in the morning. And of course, I will say everything, but not now. Robert got up, went to the bathroom now, put it down now, and please don't be angry.

Bobby cut the line by saying this, but still, Richie was calling him, and he was forced to switch off his mobile.

Mithun and Ananta are making various plans together from midnight. Leader Jeet Roy and his team have come home with threats, and the way they did before is completely blocked, so now he is busy discovering new routes. The houses far away are quiet and quiet, everyone is asleep. But in Mithun's own closed dark room, they are spending the night awake with two drunks. And there is a too criminal message and those who have the unrefined air of burning poison in their hearts, to which hate and demonic lust are rising.

Mithun said to Ananta, "Well, it would be fun if we both kidnapped Nisha from the street, raped her and then killed her and destroyed the evidence, you know? I went crazy to crush her pride, Ananta? I, I can't be patient anymore. Is it possible to force it?"

Mithun, you will be in danger if make such a hasty decision. If you do something to her now or if something happens to her, everyone will blame you first because you are now number one on the suspects' list in the public's eyes. So whatever you have to do now, you have to plan with a very cool head.

Why? They also killed your sister Lesa. What could you do?

We had to accept their rate with a lot of money. And you all know, it was too late for us to find out the truth because it was a terrible accident. We learned about the incident from Nayan Aunty much later that night, and Nayan Aunty is a poor man, just like us, so she didn't want to be a witness in this case. And no matter how big the truth, the crime cannot be proved without witnesses. But your point is very different, so I'm telling you for your own good.

Why? Does my father lack money or not? What a coward! I won't let the case go to court.

You don't understand, you're completely blind. Nisha is a very clever and educated girl, so she has brought all your incidents to the public's notice and has come home and warned you till Jeet. Then with her again. If you do too much, Mr Jeet will kill you. Do you know him? A very terrible man. And I'm not in it. Whatever you do, will do at your own risk. I will sleep now. You said so I came to rest at your house. Otherwise, I would not have come. My mom's body is not good. You sleep, we'll think tomorrow morning, let's see what can be done.

Yes, you are right. Find a way

OK, OK, I will.

Yes, you have to think about me. If not, your salary is off this month.

Ananta doesn't answer this question.

The two fell asleep with their faces covered on both sides. Then it was three o'clock at night. On the other hand, Richie was shocked by Bobby's behaviour today, and the pillow got wet with the tears.

16.

At dawn, a new sunrise painted in bright blue lines far away in the blue sky for another day. Last night all the sleeping birds started chirping and flew out for the rest of the day. The story begins again,

Richie is fast asleep, just like a tired body after late nights of terrible crying. She didn't get up at eight o'clock in the morning. She responded to her mom Nila's call and sat up.

Why so much sleep? Don't go to the office? It's at eight o'clock. When to go? Are you OK?

Yes, mom. I won't go to the office today. Where is Clifton?

Why? He is still asleep.

Hmmm. I have a severe headache, and I feel like I have a fever. And I have to make a monthly report in two days, so I'm thinking of bringing the medicine with him. I will eat only if I feel very bad or not.

Well. Get up, I'm calling him. And I'm heating the tea, drink it.

Richie's younger brother Clifton went to the market with money from her. And in the morning, Richie spread out a bundle of papers all over the bed and sat down to make a report. Because most of her salary is spent on running the family. Now his brother Francis has bought a place in the city and has reduced the amount of money he has to send monthly. So in a poor family, money is a precious thing where emotions like nightmares, tears, pride, anger, upset, love, affection are sometimes very insignificant. Still, without knowing it, the page of her papers was getting wet with tears dripping from her eyes. Today she will no longer call Bobby. After reaching so many times in the night that he switches off his mobile phone without talking, then what right will she call him? So she remained silent, that silence is better today. But still, why is her weak mind checking the message again and again without knowing it, no, Bobby didn't send any message. Bobby, no calls yet. Alas! The heart is torn.

It was about nine o'clock in the morning, and Bobby got up, washed his hands, and had breakfast.

Bobby called Neha first, his First Love and now that another fascination has come and sat on his mind because his ex-girlfriend will be the mother of his child. Moreover, Richie's innocent and straightforward love seemed to lighten with the irresistible curiosity to know yesterday's unfinished words with Neha. Bobby called Neha. From the other side came the long, sweet voice, "Hello Bobby. I've been waiting for your call since that morning. I knew you would call me, did you?"

Hmm, what do you want to say?

What can I say again? You said that will tomorrow.

Hmmm

I wonder if I have anything left to say, Bobby. I told you all my words last night.

Well. Then keep it now.

Why? Don't you like talking to me now?

Not really, now I'll call Richie, you know? When we talked last night, she called me many times while I was talking to you. It was late at night, and I didn't speak to her anymore. I think she is furious. So now I'll call her.

"OK." Neha put down the phone.

Who knows what Bobby understood? Now there is no time to understand, meanwhile, Richie is in extreme trouble. Bobby called Richie once, twice, three times, many times, nonstop, but she didn't answer. No, it looks like she won't answer the call—message after message. Butt got no answer.

Meanwhile, whenever there is silence on the screen of Richie's mobile, Bobby is calling, Richie is staring at the screen, and then the clouds of Richie's arrogance are crying again and again. Richie's account books are somehow getting wet with tears.

And so Bobby called Neha again to share Richie's sadness of not answering the call. But what a wonderful thing! Now Neha is not answering her call.

For the first couple of times, Bobby thought he was wrong, thinking that Neha might be too busy at work so maybe she wasn't getting time to call. But no. It was late in the morning, but neither of them answered Bobby's call today. Neha was so upset with Bobby's behaviour that she wanted to teach him and didn't answer his call.

This is what happens when you step on two boats.

Rakesh came at noon. Bobby lay at home, "What happened, Bobby? Are you upset?"

No.

Won't you go to the field today?

I won't, Rakesh. You're welcome. Can you bring me some wine? Being very intoxicated.

You sit at home and drink wine! If your father knew, I wouldn't have a job anymore.

Damn. I will eat quietly and lie down. Dad doesn't know. Besides, I won't live, Rakesh, my state of mind is evil. Dad is no longer at home.

Bobby, it would be doomed if he knew. So be very careful.

Yes, I'm careful you bring it. Take the money.

Damn, I have stock. I have stockpiled the car in a secret place, so no worries. Wait a minute.

Rakesh quietly hid everyone's eyes and brought a wine bottle and a packet of chips for Bobby. He went and came. The frantic, reckless Bobby closed the door and started drinking that bitter nectar, glass after glass. His body was completely taken away, so he lay down on the soft bed of the beautiful bed with the money bought by his father's hard work. Yet happiness and peace are not getting anything. That is why people say that joy and peace are scarce things.

Meanwhile, Mithun's friend and employee Ananta came home early in the morning, then went to Dharmanagar market and brought some fresh vegetables and a fish. And his mother is pleased, how many people in the food alliance with the son's income? Ananta has seen from his childhood that their family has only poverty and boundless deprivation, complaints. To fight this poverty, Lesa has gone to work in the house of a rich man like Mr Patrick and has passed away prematurely. It can be said that the earth has been freed from irritation. So now there are only three. Her father is a perpetual patient, so he spends her days and nights in bed. However, he has been friends with marijuana since birth. And he goes to a hall near this Dharmanagar city and gets addicted to cannabis. Otherwise, the rest of the time, he had unnecessary quarrels, fights and even fights with his mother. Besides, he never had any action. It is a matter of great regret, but this is the eternal truth. Lesa doesn't survive in the world today because of this nature of Ananta's father. Whoever goes there doesn't return, only the memories have given by her, and the amount of grief is endless.

So even today, Ananta's mother cries silently for Lesa. Mother is always the mother.

It was going to be late afternoon, but Ananta didn't come home. He went to the market in the morning. After losing one child, the mother's only concern is for another child. He is sitting on the porch of a mud hut with a broken thatched roof. Anjana Devi is just waiting and waiting, when does Ananta come? Immediately he came in, and his mother's outburst erupted, and Ananta immediately said, "Why are you so worried, mom? I don't understand. There were a lot of delivery dates. I did so it was late. "

Her mother was happy, "It's so much. Now take a bath and come for lunch. I haven't eaten yet. I'm waiting for you."

Why are you waiting for me?

He took a quick bath. His mother decorated very nicely and put thick white rice, vegetables, and fish in front of him.

Ananta ate and said to his mother, "Did Dad eat?"

Yeah, He ate and went out to his work.

However, even after a long time, a sad smile of longing has appeared on the face of this tragic mother today. Anjana is not very old, but in just forty-five years, her hair has turned white in the battle of Life.

Ananta said, "You know, mom, I have earned extra two hundred rupees today, you save it. And I have some money tomorrow, I will eat it and go to the market, you know? I will bring medicine for you right now. Yesterday you had a fever, still cooking. If it weren't for today's work, I would have cooked."

Yes, will you cook and feed me now? Is that all it is left? Crazy one.

Yes, I could cook. You sit next to me and teach me.

Bobby fell asleep after swallowing alcohol, his older brother Robbie, younger brother Robert came out the door to shout a lot. But the awful smell of alcohol coming out of the body could no longer be covered. Robert realised and left in silence. The reason is straightforward, he also drinks alcohol himself. But outside this house. But now Bobby is a convicted felon for drinking at home.

Meanwhile, Bobby's mother, Kalpana Devi, has been sitting with food since then and is always calling.

There is no time to eat Mr Patrick now. Because of the election. He left home long ago to spend time on political work.

Robbie said to Bobby, "Bobby, did you drink alcohol?"

Bobby said, "Yeah. I ate by mistake." Bobby bowed his head like a criminal and stood in front of his Robbie with a turbulent body.

Robbie's mind is very soft, and he loves his brothers very much. So to deal with this situation, Bobby said softly, "Go and take a bath now. The stench is coming out of your body. Come to eat with a little perfume and powder." Robbie went out.

17.

Bobby slept again after eating. It is getting evening, but Bobby didn't wake up. No more talking to Richie.

At that time, Mr Patrick is at home, along with his three sons. At half-past eight in the night, a group of people outside the house seems to be having trouble with something. Someone is shouting Mr Patrick's name too loudly, so Mr Patrick and his family come out. Many people came, like a sea of people.

About five hundred people in front of the main gate of their house. They don't look like their own people, but everyone is their neighbour. But Mr Patrick doesn't understand why such an arrival. He asks fluently in front of them, "What's the matter? Why are you shouting so much?"

One of the crowd came out and say, "You take care of your boys first. Take care of your family first, and then you will come to contest the election. Otherwise don't."

Mr Patrick, who has been a Member of Parliament for fifteen years, is shocked today. To this day, no one has been able to speak in front of him like this. Or didn't dare to say. But what happened today? Why does he hear such things? Why it is so mysterious? Mr Patrick say, "What happened? What did my sons do?"

Another saying from the crowd, "What did them not do? And you are hiding everything. Why did?"

Mr Patrick again says in a very humble tone, in the face of the indignation of the five hundred people, and then politely says, "Why? What has any of my sons doing? Tell me a little clearer. I will judge with the appropriate punishment for that crime."

All the members of Mr Patrick's family are standing there like deaf and dumb. Because they are about five hundred, and they are all twenty or twenty-two.

Robbie is trembling with fear, Bobby also stands with his head down. However, Robbie has little courage. He comes forward to speak on behalf of the father, "What have I done?"

Suddenly another says, "We have nothing to do with you. Your younger brother, Robert, is a characterless, lustful person. Can you deny it? Can any of you answer, why did Lesa die?"

The truth that is kept under wraps should be heard from the agitated crowd like accountability on the face. They never thought of it. Robbie can't find the answer anymore, because, in the group, he unknowingly saw Anjana Devi, the mother of their housemaid Lesa. Robbie really can't find a direct response to this. He becomes speechless and remains silent. But Robert burst to cover his guilt, saying, "Who died? Is it our responsibility to find out? And I did nothing."

As soon as Robert lied in front of the excited crowd, one of the group shouts, "This piglet ruined a girl's Life and denying it again today? Aren't you talking too much?"

Immediately another says, "If you talk more, I'll kick my shoes to your face, bastard."

One of them says, "The club has turned the house into a drunken hangout place only for him."

Another says, "Yes, the bastard has grown too much. Hold him ... hold him ... hold him."

Robert also bravely take two steps in front of them and says in his mouth, "Who dares to put his hand on me? Third class people?"

As soon as Robert abused them, some people come toward him, and another grabbed the collar of his shirt and throw him on the ground. Then they started beating, slapping, kicking and punching his chest on his back like a DJ. It's called mass whitewashing. "

As soon as Bobby saw his beloved brother's misery and went ahead to remove Robert from them, the excited crowd again got another drum called Bobby and began to play mercilessly. Let it burst, they have a feeling like there is no problem.

Seeing the situation worse, Mr Patrick and his calm eldest son escape from there and enter the house. They enter the house, lock the door and sit down. Meanwhile, Kalpana Devi and the women of her home keep crying and saying,

"Leave them alone. They will die. Forgive them. Oh, God, save them. Leave them, leave them."

On the one hand, the sound of slapping, beating is going on and on the other hand, the sound of crying. Mr Patrick goes to his room, lock the door, and begin to tremble not finding a way. So he calls Faithful youth leader Jeet Roy and then the police also. Robbie goes to the next room and calls Jolie to tell her everything. Because Jolie's father Mrinal Master is a close friend of Mr Patrick and an executive member of the same party. The excited crowd outside the house ignored the women, and everyone is busy entering the house. Everyone is saying, "Where did Patrick go? Why don't you see him? Where is the old man? Take him. Let's go inside the house." When everyone left these two brothers and started entering the house, a black Jip came and stopped there. And from that car, a young man, covered in black cloth from head to toe, jumped out with an SLR (Self Loading Rifle) in his hand.

He jumps and fires three shots into the air. All become silent, and from that car, a group of fifteen armed men suddenly come down with their weapons, some with light machine guns, and some with carbine machine guns. It's like a well-equipped battalion coming out to fight on the Lock Cargill Border. And the red-haired man raises a barrel of the gun in his hand and says to the five hundred people, "Hey, Mr Oni's pet dogs, I will shoot to your head at if you go forward to Mr Patrick's house. You have to be ashamed, you don't have the power to compete for elections, so you have come to lose by getting dirty like this. Who will go forward? "

Realising the situation is favourable, Mr Patrick and Robbie come out of the house, and after a while, the people dispersed and begins to run away. All are silent in an instant.

Today's angel is Jeet, Jeet Roy. And the battalion is his own so that he would never have to retreat in the oncoming war. Today, it has been used to protect Mr Patrick's honour and their party leader's honour.

Mr Patrick took them to his own house, although they are all familiar to him. Mr Patrick says, "Jeet, I didn't realise that such a thing could happen in a hurry. What A horrible thing! I can't think."

Jeet says, "My father was shot dead by the police. You can say we have family records so I have learned to be ready for any storm, uncle."

Good. Good. You have shown a lot of foresight today. Great. It's cracking. I saw how everyone fled in fear of you. But I didn't think Oni would fight such a dirty battle to win the election. You know what?

Jeet said, "Yes, he can do everything. And in the future, they will do even more heinous things Just to win the election. It is just such a trailer." Jeet gives a smile.

Immediately the police come. And Mr Patrick shouted at the police.

Jeet then selectively sued Mr Oni's party leadership in the name of a few locals. Then the police left after completing the investigation. Jeet and his forces also.

Twelve o'clock at night, the whole house is quiet. After a while, Bobby and Robert's screams come from their room. Their family doctor came and gave primary treatment to the two brothers. Now they will have continuous bed rest for a month.

Now, except Robbie, his other two brothers broke their arms and legs and lay on the bed. On the other hand, Richie heard all the incidents from her younger brother Clifton and calls Bobby.

18.

Hello, Richie?

Yes, how are you now?

Not much better. There is severe pain all over the body, nose, mouth and eyes are all swollen, you can't recognise now.

Why? What happened?

I went to save Robert, so they also beat me. My body is in excruciating pain, and I can't look me in the eye. So swollen?

Why? You didn't take pain medication?

I ate. The pain subsided for a while, and now it has started again. Richie, what happened to my body, do you understand? I won't live?

What are you saying?

I'm right. Will understand when you see me. If I won't be sent to the nursing home tomorrow. I won't live. I won't live anymore.

So why are you still at home? You all need to be sent to a nursing home.

One of the biggest problems is that if we two brothers are admitted to the nursing home today, my father's opener Mr Oni will be pleased to the run-up to the elections. So my dad thinks that the treatment will be in all families, not in nursing homes or hospitals.

Well understood. Do what feels right. Here, what else can I say?

Yes, let's see what happens. Now I will sleep a little. I can't wait anymore. Being very uncomfortable in the body. Nothing looks good.

OK, sleep but with the correct answer to one last question...

Yes, what?

Who were you talking to last night?

Hey, are you still in that? When I forgot, it was Neha. Her husband bought the phone. So......

Pu ... Pu ... Pu.... Busy tone.

Again calling.

Switch off.

A few days passed, Jolie fell off Robbie's sari and sit on the back of his bike. Who knows what suddenly changed her mind. Jolie said to Robbie, "Robbie, let's go somewhere else." Robbie immediately agreed.

They went out in the morning with a tidy dress up—the dense jungle of the rain forest on both sides and the road in the middle of it.

Now at ten o'clock in the morning, they arrive at their target Teesta Barrage. Robbie goes to stand the bike in the right place, and Jolie gets busy fixing her messy hairs flying in the air of the moving motorcycle. She took out a small mirror from the bag and looked at the condition of her face. She also takes care of the sari.

They sit in two chairs facing each other at the table in the middle. Robbie has been staring at Jolie since then. This time Jolie says, "What are you looking at from there? Your eyes don't look good."

Why? What's in my eye?

Evil eye.

Evil! Where to say well, isn't it?

Why did you bring me here, Robbie? To see the excellent look?

You are not a little romantic, you are good at figuring out the opposite of everything.

Oh, being so romantic before marriage can be very harmful, so be careful. Got it?

What could be the harm to you? Am I a harmful mosquito, or will I bite you?

Hmmm. You are a more harmful animal than him, would it be better if it was a mosquito?

Meanwhile, the waiter says, "What are you going to eat?"

"Let's see Menu," Jolie said. "We will order later."

Robbie said, "Eat. Eat whatever you like."

Why are you feeding me?

What? I will feed you, all your Life.

Full Life is different, now it is a little different.

Why? What is so different now?

There is. There is. I'm not here to empty your pockets. I didn't feel right reading continuously. So I come to visit.

That's good. Now, why not eat something again?

You are a fool. Have I ever said not to eat? Don't listen to the ears? I said I won't eat with your money.

Then who will pay the bill? Who else is here except me?

I am. I will eat with my own money plus I will feed you. You paid for the bike oil, and I will pay for food—equal.

I can't take you anymore. Why did I fall in love with you?

Feeling sorry too? Then you can go. I won't be stuck.

Why did it come to leave?

Didn't? Then it is perfect. Stay here, stay.

What else will Robbie talk about with this Jolie? The whole romantic mood was ruined. While eating, Jolie suddenly looked at the table in front of them and saw that Ananta and Mithun, the boys from their area, we're also eating. Jolie's eyes fell with Ananta. As soon as Ananta finishes eating, he comes to them, "Jolie, have you come here to visit?"

Hmm, Ananta. You?

We often do. Let's deliver the goods.

Oh.

So we usually eat here.

Robbie played the food with attention but quietly listened to the two of them with more attention. And during the trouble, that day, Ananta's mother's eyes met his eyes, and he remembered. And for the sin committed by Robert, a blood brother in his own mother's womb, Robbie was feeling very ashamed today. Ananta looked at Robbie and said, "Robbie?"

Yes.

Can I tell you something?

"Yes, tell freely." And Robbie's mind was just beating, wouldn't he go to the context of the death of his sister Lesa? Jolie is here again. Then defeat, if he says something like that in front of Jolie, all honour will be lost.

Ananta smiled a little and said, "Robbie, Jolie is very comfortable with you. Will you invite me if you get married?"

Shall I invite? You have a lot of work to do. You are the son of the house next to mine.

"I will do it, Ravi, I will do all your work. My sister also used to do a lot of work in your house." And didn't say, he was stuck.

"Yes, Ananta. You are right. She had done a lot for us. But in return for what she got." Robbie also fell silent.

The two are silent.

Jolie looked at the situation strangely and said, "Ananta, what about Mithun? I heard that Nisha is very irritated."

Don't tell me anymore? I also irritate. I work as a driver in his car because of my livelihood.

What is he doing now? I saw the two of you eating together.

What else to do? Eating beer.

Aren't you eat?

No.

I have to go now, or He will be angry.

And listen, don't tell anyone that we are here. Got it?

Yes. I have to go now.

OK.

Ananta and his mother sat down to eat at night. Ananta says, "Mom, you know I talk to Robbie today."

What were you talking about?

Then he told all the incidents that happened at Teesta Barrage. At the same time, he mentioned the word given to Jolie and said not to say these words to anyone else.

Then Anjana said to the boy, "Well done, Robbie is the only good man in their house. Will talk to him when meeting him."

Well, if they invite us to his wedding, then?

Then you go. I won't go. If her parents come home and invite us, then I won't.

His mother used to come to our house. How many times a day she would send the news to call Lesa to work in their home. Used to come many times before. Comes now like back?

No. Doesn't come then. Not a single day comes. Now Lesa is not there, so they are not needed.

All right. We won't go either. Don't we have the honour of being poor? But mother, what if Mr Patrick comes to our house and invites us?

Let's see. Eat now.

CHARACTERLESS

The day before the election, the vote is after the night. Today, there is a lot of food being served in different places, all those who have been working day and night for the increase of votes are being fed a good meal today. Jeet Roy has brought the whole fifty thousand rupees from Mr Patrick telling it. Jeet makes the arrangement then he left and said he would come at night.

Delicate basmati rice sacks, they are being washed into the rice. The smoke of hot rice and its aroma are all around. Five goats were brought, along with the butcher. The red blood-stained meat cut in their hands is being collected in big bowls. They are washed and mixed with raw, alluring foods like onion, dried chili paste, garlic, ginger paste, turmeric paste, and a tin of oil. Which is called marinade. Lots of people. Everyone has put their hands to work, no one is sitting, and today is everyone's happy day.

Large pots, pans, Gamla, cooking, dancing, singing, rejoicing, merriment, wine, marijuana, and cigarettes are furnished in this open courtyard. The air of intoxication, the aroma of rice and the smell of meat all around.

Everyone sat down to eat. It's at midnight. Jeet and Mr Patrick came together.

19.

Mr Patrick came in front of them, Jeet standing behind him. Mr Patrick said, "How's the food? Can you eat happily?"

"Yes" all at once.

"Very good. Well done." Another replied with putting a giant lump of rice in his mouth.

"Great, what I'm eating, I can't tell, what a taste!" someone else told him. But the red oil broth of meat was rolling by the side of his chin, he overlooked that.

Mr Patrick smiled a little at the way he ate. "There's rice on all sides of your chin." He said. "Eat Happily. And do you remember the real thing?"

Yes, remember. You don't have to worry.

That's the diameter. But this time it is different.

Mr Patrick said to a man called Halan again, "Halan, Did you get the food, right?"

Yeah, I overate. My stomach has become very heavy. Look, I can't stand up. I think my stomach will burst.

Mr Patrick says, "Sit down, and you don't have to get up. There is still food left on your plate. Finish eating."

I will return home only after eating all, right?

Well, very well, you don't have to go home. Will go home after voting.

OK, so be it.

The meal ended at three in the night.

After sleeping for three hours, everyone came to vote again in groups at six in the morning. Huge line. Jeet had arranged for a car to bring the old men and women to vote. So that not a single confirmed vote counted is left out. They also came. Everyone came.

After all, voting ended without any problem. Police were deployed, and in the evening, the polling officer came and took everything.

On the other hand, Mr Oni was no less than Mr Patrick in these events.

The vote is over then. Now there is no discussion about elections. What used to be an open discussion has now turned into a whisper. But no matter which team wins, these ordinary people will join that team.

Bobby stretched his legs and lay down for a few days. He was taken to the bathroom with the help of Rakesh. Robert is now kept in a separate room.

At noon, Bobby had just eaten rice, sitting cross-legged on the bed. Rakesh is always busy helping him.

But Bobby is distraught. Because neither Richie nor Neha has called since that incident. Even though he called countless times, they didn't have any response. "Rakesh, can you give me some beer today?"

Are you upset? Nothing can be given to you now.

"Why?" Bobby asked helplessly.

Your father is at home, can't you see??

So what happened?

He has been coming and seeing you, and now he is doomed if he smells alcohol. He will cut me into pieces and float me in the Teesta water.

Want to drink beer, so much trouble for it.

Where did I disturb? You are giving me as much trouble. You have been shouting 'eat beer' for three days.

What do I do then? I don't feel well.

So what do I do? He said again, "Hey! I haven't been able to have fun with my sweethearts for a long time. It's all for you. You take medicine now and go to sleep. I'll go to the bathroom. I have diarrhoea, I can't eat properly. I heard your mother cooked swan egg soup again."

Who said that?

I saw Neomi going to the kitchen in the morning with a lot of eggs. Needless to say, I sensed myself, what a beautiful fragrance.

That didn't give me that, I ate horn fish soup without salt and spices.

Yes, it's notable for your two sick brothers. Not for us.

"Why?" Asked very disappointed.

I don't know, the doctor said.

Maybe so.

Now lie down quietly. You are talking too much, keep quiet. The ears are ringing.

Bobby lay down quietly, Rakesh said again." Come on, let's get out of the bathroom first, and then eat. I'm dying of stomach ache." Rakesh ran towards the bathroom.

A well across a lot of space next to the kitchen, the bathroom next to it. The bathroom door closed from the inside, so Rakesh knocked on the door.

Immediately, "Who?" Their work girl, Neomi.

"I, Rakesh, have diarrhoea. It's very stressful. Get out soon, or I'll have a bandage on my pants." Said with incredible difficulty.

On hearing this, Neomi hurriedly opened the door and came out and looked at Rakesh as if swallowing and said "the crazy one. Appears wherever I go. There is no peace even when I come to the bathroom."

Rakesh has been entered in the bathroom, and he sat quietly listening to Neomi. Because now it is more important to clean the stomach than to argue. Swan egg soup, ah, must be eaten. Again in the hands of Neomi. There is no profit in arguing.

The shadow shouted from outside, "Hey Rakesh, now I have entered the bathroom next door. To take a bath. Don't disturb me" She rushed into the next bathroom.

Two minutes later, the bathroom singer sang while taking a bath in the next bathroom. On the other hand, even though Rakesh finished, he was sitting and listening to the song. Because this is the place for Neomi, Naveen, Rakesh, to take rest. No one will disturb.

Meanwhile, Kalpana Devi called out loudly, "Neomi, Neomi?"

The bathroom singer stopped the song and responded by shouting, "Aunty, I'm in the bathroom."

How long will you stay in the bathroom? It's been a long time, come back soon. I'm going to feed Robert.

"OK, coming." She roared, and in a shallow voice, she kept saying to himself, "I don't like this job anymore, I don't have money, but there is no peace even when I come to the bathroom. Always, Neomi? Neomi? Why do you have to do the job of sending food to Naveen? She won't do it? Lesa is dead, and I am dead now. Am I less beautiful? I am getting married now, will I have a beautiful family with my husband and children. Will the groom caress me day and night? I understand everything. I won't have a family in this Life. "The voice of the throat is full of sorrow.

Don't know if God heard, but Rakesh, who was sitting in the bathroom next door, listened. This time Rakesh came out and came to her bathroom and said in a shallow voice, "Yes, yes, all your hopes will be fulfilled." Then he fled.

Neomi hurried out of the bathroom, looking from side to side for Rakesh.

20.

Neomi shone around the well as far as the eye could see. No, Rakesh is nowhere around. But she whispered that he didn't hear all the secret personal words?

Neomi wears a large yellow-necked shirt, and black pants and a red scarf are wrapped around the neck so that it is not difficult to work. Naveen came to the well, to wash his hands, now is the time to eat. If the owners eat, they will be called.

Naveen.

Washing his muddy feet, he said, "yes."

Did you see Rakesh standing here?

No, I just came, right in front of you, didn't you see?

No. I didn't see you.

Why? Do you have eye problems? Tell Kalpana Aunty, you have to see a doctor. How will you work if you don't see?

The shadow became furious and said to Naveen, "Do people just call you a flock of sheep? Did I ask? And do you understand? As a human being, you are useless."

Am I crazy? Are you abusing me? I will complain to Aunty in your name. I will say that you have called me a dog.

Damn. Who did I go to ask? I've lost all sense of humour. "

From the kitchen again Kalpana shouts and calls to Neomi, and immediately the shadow runs a hundred meters at full speed.

Kalpana cooks food for everyone from the owner of the house to the servant. She has done so even today because what she gives to whom she doesn't offer to others follows his very personal constitutional rules. However, the addition or subtraction as recommended is the constitution of this given food list.

Now she sent food to Robert's room by Neomi. The shadow also came out with food at lightning speed. Mr Patrick and his eldest son Robbie are sitting at the dining table next to their kitchen.

On the other hand, their grandmother Anila and Mr Patrick's father, Mrigen, are about ninety-five years old. They can't sit and eat as tall as a camel at such a high dining table. So the two are sitting side by side to get a seat on the floor.

Kalpana is sitting in a chair and feeding them, and Neomi is giving them a bowl of rice, veg Mudgal, vegetables, duck egg soup, and salad. And Kalpana Devi is providing them without any problem.

The old woman sitting on the floor was given white rice and oil, salt, cooked with fewer spices, easy to digest, thin broth of horn fish and a little dal in the bowl. Eating fried food is strictly forbidden. The old man still doesn't have a single tooth. The old man mumbled and said to Neomi, "I saw the egg cooked today, didn't?"

Immediately Neomi said, "Who said the egg is cooked? The egg is not cooked. Eat with this fish."

What will happen if the digestive capacity of the old man is reduced? The taste of the tongue is not lost. Then the old woman also gave him a threat, so he started eating quietly.

On the other side, Mr Patrick, who was eating at the table, said to Robbie, "How are Jolie?"

Good.

Is she willing to marry you?

I think so.

"Why? You don't confirm?"

No, I mean

What do you mean? If she agrees, tell me, the election is over now. I've been free for a few days, now I talk to her father. I need to know before that, whether Jolie agrees?

Yeah, seems to agree. But she doesn't say anything clearly. She only told that she won't get married without finishing graduation.

That's good. Let her finish her studies first. And is it OK that you go to their house every day?

No, where did I go every day?

"You know how long you've been there? But the news that you're going to go around with her comes to me. I keep all the news, Robbie, but I don't like it at all." He got up because he had finished eating.

Kalpana sent rice to Naveen by Neomi and gave everything, but didn't provide eggs.

She was going to give eggs for Rakesh, but Neomi stopped her. sHe said that Rakesh had diarrhoea. So all foods come to them, but the eggs were left in front of them.

Naveen and Rakesh sit under a tree in the outer yard and eat. Naveen started eating what he got in his stomach like a hungry boy. But before Rakesh could look at food, he bent down and went to look for something else through the gap in the neck of Neomi's shirt that was feeding him. But he was not lucky, the binding of the veil was quite strong. But when he didn't see the swan's egg on the plate, he said in a frustrated voice, "The egg wasn't cooked today, Neomi?"

What if? Eat what I have given you.

No, I just wanted to know, that's why you stay in the kitchen.

"Yes, I do." she widened his eyes. Then again in a grave voice, she replied clearly, "I am not the owner, and those who have diarrhoea are forbidden to eat eggs." The last face went away with the hematite.

By this time Rakesh understood quite well, who is the main culprit of not getting eggs? Neomi took revenge for the bathroom. "If I have not taken revenge for stopping eating eggs, then I am not Rakesh Gupta," Rakesh swore in his mind.

Many nights, Bhutan's means of communication with India is National Road. No. 31, the place is Changrabandha. There is a three-bigha corridor in the distance, India and Bangladesh's border, and there is a famous ancient brothel, so maybe it has got such a name.

Mithun still could not stand on the ground as he had been drinking heavily. He always wanted to do sex, so after doing all these, many nights passed and Ananta was sleeping in the truck by the side of the road.

Mithun came and shouted, "Open the door."

As soon as Ananta got up and opened the truck's door, Mithun tried his best to come upon his own but could not. Ananta looking down at the situation. He pushed him very hard and lifted him. Meanwhile, Mithun was going through a flood of insults, and Ananta was listening in silence. There is no way without listening to him.

As soon as Ananta was about to start the car, Mithun said, "I will drive, I will drive my car, and you don't have to drive anymore."

Why? What did I do? And you can't move now. How do you drive? This is the highway.

Shut up, shut up. Are you giving me knowledge? Will you teach me? I'll kill you right now and throw you out of the car.

No matter what Mithun said, he didn't dare to hold the steering wheel. So Ananta sat quietly in the driver's seat. And he said, "Tell me, what happened to you? If you don't tell me, how will I understand? Since then, you have been abusing."

I told you to make a plan, did you?

Yes.

What have you done? Tell me? Tell me what you have planned. Nisha insulted me and left, were you standing and watching the scene?

No, I have a perfect plan for you.

Say, say. I can't adjust right now with anyone but Nisha, understand?

Got it, but I'm thinking of one thing.

What are you thinking?

Can you do exactly what I said?

I can. I can do everything. You just say it once.

When all ways are closed, only one way is open.

What is that way? Tell me quickly, I can't be patient anymore. If you can make tonight.

No, I don't have the wisdom to do something so fast.

Well, then I'll have a little patience. Still, I want her. No one's got her. I can't think.

Got it,

Two large holes in the front, not repaired for a long time. The condition of this road was horrible, yet Ananta was avoiding it as much as possible, saving it, driving the car slowly and at the same time calming the drunken Mithun was a much more challenging task than this moment.

Tell me, tell me quickly.

Not now.

On the other hand, someone secretly came to Mr Patrick's house that night to give him a report, although the news could have been given over the phone. Come to say there was a particular need.

And Bobby couldn't stay up all night. And he thought to himself, the one who truly loves him will indeed receive the call when she can no longer stay. Otherwise, reply to the message.

21.

Richie is lying alone in bed that night, repeatedly fidgeting side by side and watching Bobby's call. Bobby is calling again and again. Has made nearly a thousand calls in these few days. The message also, "Please, Richie, please listen." And the substantial clouds of her pride began to flow like a torrent of water with two eyes, like rain, a rough sea. And in her mind, like the white cotton clouds of autumn, Bobby's memories floated in the sky, dancing with her. She can't do it anymore. And every moment the stone of his pride was shattering. And she's going to say to herself, "Bobby, what did I do? Can you tell? Why did you cheat on me so much? Why did you go back to Neha?" And I gave you all my heart, body and soul, is it worth nothing? Yet you could do that? If this is his ultimate reward? Maybe that's what I deserved. Now, why are you calling me again and again? Do you have anything left to do? Stop, Bobby. Stop your random calling. I can't anymore, Bobby. Looks like you'll calm down when I'm dead. So be it, be it my death, yet you find peace. OK, let's see what you mean, but this is the last chance." Thinking about this, she sent a short message to Bobby, "midnight now, we'll talk tomorrow."

Bobby had just received a message from Richie after all this time. As soon as he got it, he said 'Hurray' in ecstasy and jumped up. Immediately the obstruction of the foot started pulling on the cracked bone. Extreme excruciating pain, Bobby cried out in pain, "Oh God." Both his parents rushed from the next room, and Rakesh got scared, got up from the bed and sat down. 'What happened? Everyone has the same question.

Bobby faced a different situation, forgot the pain and said, "No, nothing happened to me, you go to sleep."

"Then why did you shout so loudly?" Mr Patrick said.

"I just ran away wondering what happened," said Kalpana.

"I'm scared too, Bobby. Tell me what happened." Rakesh said.

"I had a terrible dream, so," Bobby said.

Everyone was relieved, reassured him with a couple of comforting good-natured words, and fell asleep again. Bobby eagerly waited for the dawn of the new sunrise and slowly fell asleep.

Mithun, on the other hand, continues to annoy Ananta terribly, always. Ananta tried to convince him in various ways but to no avail.

Ananta was driving the car with significant inattention while trying to convince Mithun in this situation. He didn't get a chance to pay attention to the vehicle And Mithun is continuously saying the same thing to his ears all the time, "Nisha, Nisha, plan, plan". Whose mood is right in this situation? Ananta is still trying hard to pay attention to both sides. While climbing the Teesta Bridge, he was hit by a big truck. The front glass of the car breaks with the sound of cracking. Ananta is knocked out of the car window and lost his sense Mithun lies unconsciously in the Truck. And does that deadly Truck stand at that spot? Fled away.

Ten minutes later, Ananta regained his sense, got into the car with great difficulty and splashed water on Mithun's face. But his own body is wounded, bloody. Still, like a brave man, he was taking out broken pieces of glass one by one from Mithun's body and crying. He said, "Hey, hey, hey, open your eyes, Mithun, Nothing happened to you, you see, nothing happened to me. Look Mithun. Get up and look me, nothing has happened to us. We are alive."

Ananta said again, "What shall I do now?" Mithun was repeatedly shaken but still didn't regain consciousness. So he put his hand on the car's steering wheel, yes the vehicle immediately proved to be alive. And Ananta didn't wait a moment, his car was speeding through the darkness and silence of that night. Ananta thought, now somehow Mithun has to go to the hospital first. And Ananta keeps calling Mithun again and again, but there is no response from Mithun.

Mithun was hospitalised that night, and Ananta was discharged after first aid. But Ananta didn't leave Mithun. So Ananta stayed with him all night to take care of him and called Mithun's house and told them all the incidents to get there very soon.

"Mithun will need blood. But his blood group will have to be tested first." Said the nurse.

"Where can I get blood?" Infinity said.

I have informed the blood bank. They will come tomorrow morning.

Well, hurry up.

Where is his guardian?

For now, I'm his guardian.

I see you are sick too.

No, I'm fine.

Jeet, after leaving Mr Patrick's house, was returning home in his jip alone in the night. Late at night, no one was anywhere, on-road of the village. The car was moving. Empty fields on both sides and a house far away in the distance are piled up like dark sculpted bodies. But everyone sleeping, silent, quiet, calm. The thorny bushes along the road are scattered here and there.

Before he could cross the road in front of Dharmanagar High School, two shots were fired targeting him which went by the side of his ear. They hit the school building wall on the side of the road, and he drove fast and reached home.

Now, after such a terrible event at night, he could not sleep. Who attacked him fatally? Who is his biggest deadly enemy?

Was he hiding in the field so late at night to shoot and kill him? So did he or they know he went to Mr Patrick's house? And he will go through this road at this time? Jeet began to spend sleepless nights obsessed with profound misery. Now just waiting for the morning. It is indecent to annoy someone so late at night.

The long-awaited morning. Another new morning.

The chirping of birds and the chirping of chickens were heard many times. And Jeet called Mr Patrick while lying on the bed. They analysed everything that happened last night from beginning to end. And a net of deep thought surrounded him.

I don't understand anything, uncle, there is a lot of tension.

Who do you suspect? Jeet?

There are many people on the list of suspects like Mr Oni, his pet terrorist Sudhir, and the case that we filed with the police at your house on the day of the incident. Didn't he do anything?

Nothing impossible. They are all on bail. One day I saw some of them in the market.

Shall I tell the police? That was a deadly attack on me.

You can. But there seems to be no gain. Will the police keep you on guard? You are such a big V.I.P. has not yet become.

That's right. But now I am terrified to go out. What to do?

It is a matter of fear. But do what you do during the day, but don't go out at night.

All right, I'll do it. But the thing that I discussed last night, what will happen to the work? That is not a day job.

Put everything off for now. Let the election results be published then. And if you can, stay in hiding for a few days, and listen, go today. Elsewhere, don't stay at home. Now understand the situation then get out. When I say, then.

Then I will leave today.

Yes, today. I see I'm doing a little research and listen to the police don't have to say these things. I will see for myself. Trust me.

Yes, uncle, there is trust. Well, then, I leave now.

Yes, get out. But in disguise. Go out dressed as a girl. Wear a sari, pull the veil so that no one can recognise you. And yes, with a bag in hand, take the revolver and money. Got it??

Got it. Can you figure out who is responsible for this deadly attack?

Of course, I can, it will take a while, but before that, I don't want any harm, and I think of you as my son, Jeet.

Get out now. I will contact you on the phone.

OK uncle

His parents, relatives and many others came to see Mithun. He has regained consciousness. However, there has been a lot of bleeding, blood has to be given. The problem here too is that his blood group is O-negative, rare blood group. Now, unfortunately, there was not a single bag in this blood bank. Surprisingly, it also matched her father's blood type. He gave blood to his son.

Ananta sat down next to Mithun's bed and said softly, "How are you now?"

He said in a shallow voice, "There is a lot of pain in the head."

All will be well, all will be well. How big is an accident hall? I am responsible for that. Mithun, forgive me.

Damn, how much I was talking to you, tell me? That's why this happened. You put my life back today. Tears welled up in the corners of his eyes. I never understood that you are so good.

Why? I'm too bad, too bad.

You didn't say the plan yesterday. Tell me now?

Again? Again the same thing.

Please tell me.

Why can't you leave Nisha? Tell me.

No girl has ever refused me except this one nightmare. So I can't accept the matter at all.

Do you want to Nisha? Tell me a little clearer?

Yes, I want a Nisha.

Then listen to my plan. Before that, I have some conditions. Tell me if you agree to it.

I agree you tell me.

Can you not drink a single day? Not to go to prostitutes? To get better? To truly love Nisha? Then I will go and tell Nisha, "Nisha, measure Mithun. He loves you." then see, and she won't be able to stay. The girl's mind. She will run to you by herself. Can you?

Hey? It became a movie. You said a great film where the villains fall in love with a girl and become a hero.

Yes, just like in the movies. Can you be a real-life hero? Can you? Can you love Nisha with your heart and soul without looking at her body?

Mithun thought for a while and said, "What did you say? Hero, real-life hero. Is there anyone?"

Why not? It can be done if you want.

Buy a cigarette, it's a headache.

Ananta was disappointed in his words. I thought, what did I propose to? The ghost remained like a ghost. "If you get Nisha, you can't smoke."

Damn, did she come here to see me? However, I will try to eliminate the intoxication of alcohol and girls. Now I won't get these in the hospital anymore.

I can't get up.

If you can get up, will drink again? Shall you go to the brothel?

No. I won't go. Still not confirmed, I will try.

Why not? It can be done if you want.

Buy a cigarette, it's a headache.

Ananta was disappointed in his words. I thought, what did I propose to? The ghost remained like a ghost. "If you get Nisha, you can't smoke."

Damn, did she come here to see me? However, I will try to eliminate the intoxication of alcohol and girls. Now I won't get these in the hospital anymore.

I can't get up.

If you can get up, will drink again? Shall you go to the brothel?

No. I won't go. Still not confirmed, I will try.

"You have to try it." Ananta was happy with her words and said, "How you will smoke? Saline in your hand."

You will burn it, I will eat.

Ananta came out to buy cigarettes for him to keep his mind.

This morning Bobby called Richie, and immediately Richie received the call, "Hello."

Hello. I know you are angry with me, but I will say that I am not what you think. I love you Richie, and you tell me what's wrong with me if Neha annoys me by calling me?

Why did you receive her call?

Did I know it was her number? She called me that night to say that she was pregnant. And hearing this good news, I was advising her to be a little more careful. And you were calling again and again.

Got it. But you could have cut her line and called me for a minute to say that you were talking to Neha on the phone for this reason.

I could tell. But you won't be angry, what was the guarantee? In the end, you got angry. You haven't received my phone for so long, didn't I have any trouble then??

Is trouble just you, Bobby?

I know you're in trouble too. But I wish you could hear me at least once.

Sorry. I don't understand, Bobby. And I didn't understand, I thought you were still in a relationship with Neha. Sorry, Bobby, I'm embarrassed.

All right. And what to do with shame?

Excuse me, Bobby. I misunderstood and suspected you. I have insulted our love too. Please forgive me.

Yes, but on one condition

What are the conditions? I agree with all your requirements.

Kiss me right now.

'Yes, umuuuuuu .. aa aa aa, now you give.

Take it, umuuuuuu .. aa aa aa .. Happy?

Yes, happy, how are you now?

Not a very good one. There is a little crack in the right leg's bone, the doctor has tied the bandage. I can't stand up on my own. I can't even walk. Do you know? Rakesh is carrying on. He is with me now.

What happened to your business?

I don't know. I think my dad is handling it.

I think so too. Your father is a very frugal man.

But my father's mind is perfect, he gives a lot to poor people.

That's right.

The day before the election, there was a huge feast.

Did you go?

No. Why should I go? Besides, I don't go anywhere.

Oooo.

As soon as he saw me, he would light a fire. Clifton was gone. I heard from him. What about your two brothers?

They are in the same condition as me—one-month full bed rest.

Well.

Why is my father angry when he sees you?

I told you before that he told me to break up with you. I didn't. That's why.

Please, don't leave me. No one will love me as much as you, Richie.

Why? Did you know today?

No, I knew that long ago. But last night I got proof of that.

Why? Were you testing?

Yes,

What were you testing?

I experimented. Rakesh is coming, we'll talk later.

Why? Where has Rakesh been for so long?

In the bathroom. He is also suffering from diarrhoea.

Bobby's mind is very bright today, as if happiness came a few decades later. As soon as Bobby cut Richie's call, Neha is calling. Now, why did Neha call again?

Bobby picked up the phone, "Hello."

22.

Jolie called Robbie and asked him to come to their house. Her parents won't be there in the afternoon. What is urgent something that cannot be said on the phone now? So Robbie explained to the two employees and went to meet Jolie in the afternoon.

Jolie was sitting in the closed room when Robbie came, she opened the door. Robbie saw the house was deserted. Great opportunity, so Robbie sat down near to Jolie's body as possible as like shameless. Jolie didn't forbid.

Robbie said, "Why do you look so beautiful today? What's the matter?"

Did I look ugly before?

No, it's not. You are always beautiful to me. Well, are you in a good mood today?

Yes, I am always OK. What's the matter with you being so romantic?

Feeling very good. Come a little closer.

I'm close, how do I get closer?

Robbie realizes the opportunity, suddenly he kisses Jolie, and removes his face before Jolie understands anything.

Jolie said, "But it didn't go well."

Shall I kiss you a little more?

Jolie blushed in shame, her body suddenly began to flow. Jolie said to him, "Robbie, will you go to the market?"

Why?

One thing to buy.

What?

Condoms.

What are you saying?

Are you shocked? Is that why you love me? Today my parents won't come home. They went to my uncle's house.

What do you say? I'll be with you tonight then.

OK. However, buy it first.

I won't go to this local market to buy condoms. Do you know? Everyone knows me as the son of Mr Patrick Chowdhury. So wait, now I go to the city by bike, then buy some more food.

Hurry up.

Robbie left and returned after a couple of hours. And on the phone, he told his father that he would stay at a friend's house in the city today. Bobby came back from town with a lot of food with condoms. The two ate together and went to bed.

Robbie filled Jolie's whole body with kisses, and her body got wet with countless kisses from head to toe. At a touch of the man's warmth, Jolie pressed him like an open mad madman and hugged him repeatedly. For the first time in Robbie's life, he got a women body and became a lion. As if chewing on him today. When he went to give a light bite, he bit it unknowingly.

"I'm in pain," Jolie said.

I can't wait anymore.

"If not, how?" Said with a laugh.

As if the two bodies merged with the two bodies and became one, nothing was left out. After one round, Robbie was lying beside her very tired, and with one of his legs on top of her, he made a pillow with Jolie's head in one of his hands, closed his eyes and was floating in the sea of extraordinary bliss. And Robbie went crazy playing with her breasts like a child. And with Robbie's lips, he was licking her ears, throat and chin. Jolie couldn't find any language, today her restless mind is calm.

Robbie said, "Why don't you say something?"

What should I say? Tell me what you want to hear.

As you wish

Will you leave me?

I'm not going anywhere without you. I love you very, very much.

Today I will tell you some truth.

What do you say?

Will you give me the correct answer to a question before that??

I will.

Who else did this to you before you did it to me?

Not with anyone, I swear.

Well, got it. But I am not a virgin. You know, I've had sex with two more before you. I tried to tell you but couldn't. I was in love with both of them, but they loved my body more than me. One of them is your younger brother Robert, now you are number three. Tell me this time, all the love for me has left your mind? If you get up, you can go too. I won't stop. Because I will think you weren't one of me, you were one of them.

Robbie pressed Jolie's mouth.

Shut up, I won't go. I'm not in love with your body. I want your body and mind, and I will marry you this month.

Robbie pressed Jolie's face.

Shut up, I won't go. I'm not in love with your body. I want your body and mind, and I will marry you this month.

Aren't you angry, Robbie, hearing the truth about losing my virginity?

Why should I be angry? You can say, hearing this truth from your mouth increased my love for you.

Robbie, will you love me like this?

Yes, this is how I will love you forever.

Will you leave me thinking of a characterless girl?

Never. But one thing.

What?

Wouldn't you leave me, go to someone else?

No. Robbie, never, I want a little love, nothing more.

Jolie, I'm awake again. Look, I'll do it again.

Do it. As long as you want, I'm just yours.

Another round went by—an ancient, primitive game of a pair of human beings in a bed. The bed is going to broke, what else?

Neha, on the other hand, called Bobby and first asked, "Hello, Bobby."

Tell me? What happened?

Nothing happened. You have been calling me so many times? Why were you repeatedly calling?

To take your news?

What will you do with my news? You should listen to Richie. Talk to Richie?

Richie in Richie's place and you are in your place.

Rakesh gestured to Bobby, who are you talking to on the phone? Bobby also gestured to Rakesh to go out a little and Rakesh left. To find the opportunity to date in the betel garden with Neomi.

He said to Neha again, "Hmm, what I was saying is that you are someone else's wife now, so I can't have any relationship with you, Jolie. No matter how much you love me, or I love you. Forget all the memories and start anew."

I never stood in your way, Bobby? Then today you are suddenly saying that.

That's not right, but you can't accept my relationship with Richie. Even if you don't say anything, I understand. I have been in love with you for a long time. I can feel all your feelings.

So, what do you mean? Tell me a little clearer?

I wish we both completely forgot about it.

I don't remember you.

Then why did you call me again with a letter?

To get rid of my childless condition because my husband won't have children, the doctor said, although he doesn't know this.

All right. Now be happy with your husband and children and listen, don't find the wrong meaning of my words. I have thoughtfully said that it will be good for both of us.

Why?

I will sleep, my body is not good.

Well, sleep.

The line was cut on both sides.

Mithun lived a miserable life lying in a hospital bed when suddenly, Nisha's father and Nisha came to see him. Unexpected. Ananta is also surprised.

Nisha's house is next to Mithun's house, a neighbour. I heard about such a big accident from Mithun's mother in the morning. So forgetting everything, they came as a neighbour. Nisha's father asked Mithun, "How are you now?"

Well, uncle, why do you come?

We came here on a reason, talked to your father on the street, and heard everything. I didn't like hearing about such an incident, so I come to see you.

But Nisha didn't say anything, she stood silently beside her father. Although Mithun was in a lot of trouble, he said to Nisha in front of Nisha's father, "Nisha, if you can forgive me, I have mistreated you."

Before Nisha could answer, her father said, "All right, you get better first. And never do what you did."

I will never do anything wrong again, uncle.

Then Nisha and her father left.

Mithun slept soundly, saw life anew, or was born again.

Ananta said to Mithun, "How are you feeling now?"

Super. When will you leave? Did the doctor say anything?

Shut up, you won't have a holiday for less than two days yet.

Who said that?

I said.

Why?

You will atone for all the sins you have committed so far by lying in this hospital bed.

Mithun laughed, "You want me to lie here? Are you a friend or an enemy?"

I am your enemy.

Then, you could have left me there. Why did you go to save my life?

Infinity finds no answer. Mithun said, "I know. What kind of enemy am I?"

Now you sleep a little.

Why? I can't sleep

You don't want to end when your chatter starts.

That's right. I'm talkative.

Yes, you are very talkative.

Well, I'm talkative. Did you notice one thing?

What?

Nisha looked like a beautiful red fairy.

No. Do you still want to go to him?

Yes, but how do I go?

After sleeping, go to meet in a dream.

"You didn't say that badly. I'll go to sleep right now," he said, closing his eyes.

A few more days passed like this. Today will give the result of the election. In the morning, Mr Patrick, his eldest son Ravi, Mrinal Master, Avinash, Clifton, and many others showed up at the counting center for him.

On the other hand, Mr Oni, Sudhir Das, Ananta Varman and many others were present. After one round of counting, Mr Oni is ahead.

23.

After another round of counting, Mr Patrick is ahead. A small smile appeared on her face, but the lines of horrible thoughts on her forehead were clearly understood. The heartbeat is rising. What happens if he loses?

The honour created by so many years of sesame seeds will be reduced to dust in an instant. No one will call him to the meeting, no one will respect him as before, no one will give him a bouquet, no one will hold an umbrella over his head, or come forward to talk.

No, that can't be. Unbeknownst to the mind, a black cloud filled the sky of thoughts. In the last round, Mr Ani is still ahead by a few votes. His condition is like having a heart attack.

Drink a glass of water, Uncle?

Jeet? When did you come?

I just came, I couldn't stay uncle. So I disobeyed your word.

But you didn't do it well. Win.

Good and evil will happen later, I saw that you have made the situation worse by sweating. Drink some water?

Is there? Give it?

After drinking a whole bottle of water, he handed her an empty bottle. And as soon as a result was announced, Mr Patrick defeated Mr Oni by a margin of ten votes.

Jeet came out and raised a thunderous slogan in response to the supporters. Mr Patrick was garlanded with roses by his supporters and Mr Oni's people left in despair.

Victory procession is going on along the main road. In front of Mr Patrick and Jeet's parade, drums are playing, the atmosphere of the festival is all around. All around the band party sound. The night is deep, now it's all cold. As if nothing happened in daylight.

The night is deep, now it's all cold. As if nothing happened in broad daylight.

The election has been over for some time. Jeet is now walking around with a swollen chest. But where? Now no one is carrying out deadly attacks. "Wonderful thing," Mr Patrick said.

I cannot think of any? Who did?

I don't know. There is a mystery.

I think so too.

So be careful, don't go too far.

Yes, uncle. But there is a profound mystery.

Yes, that's why let's open the sixth sense: politics, not boy play.

Yes, Will, I go to Mr Oni's house to do that?

Which seems to be our enemy but an intelligent enemy. The light of day won't harm you.

And take it with you??

Yes, revolver? Mast, that's your life safety. Keep it with you. What's the answer, call me and let me know.

OK.

Jeet has gone. But immediately, at noon, Arupa, Mr Patrick's poor neighbour, came and said to Mr Patrick, "Uncle, it would be beneficial to give me a house. I am terrified because I am alone with my daughter at night. "Nayan was standing next to her. She also came to Mr Patrick with the same desire.

I will. You don't have to worry, but you have to do me some for me.

What are the benefits? We voted for you.

I know.

Mr Patrick explained something and Arupa and Nayan agreed.

Robbie's marriage was arranged, Mr Patrick and Mrinal Master sat down and arranged the marriage. Jolie agreed to the wedding a long time ago for an unknown reason, but Robbie promised not to interfere with her studies. They got married a month later.

Robbie's younger brother Robert can't accept Jolie's marriage to his older brother Robbie at all. Robert came to Robbie's room and said, "I have something to talk to you about."

What do you want to say?

Didn't you find any other girl? You may not know that Jolie is a characterless girl.

Is that so?

Yes.

Who told you that Jolie is characterless? He is going to be my wife, so fix your language from now on.

"I have proof," Robert said in a loud, demonic smile and straight forward.

You won't correct in life? What proof? What evidence do you have?

You close the marriage. I have said it many times, but it is not going well. Otherwise, I will unmask his character and leave him naked in the market. Everyone will shout in the name of Jolie. That must not be good?

What evidence is there? Again saying, fix your language.

You don't follow my language. Turn on this DVD. There is all the evidence in it.

Robert left a DVD on his bed and went to his room.

Robbie stopped going to the store and watched the DVD. A terrible scene from Jolie's blue film with his brother Robert. His heart was burning, but he tried to keep calm.

Much later, I told him. I warned him a lot. I told him over and over again, "Get out of my brother's way." He didn't listen. So today I was forced to show you. And if you don't annul this marriage voluntarily, then I will be forced to publish these.

You are in that video yourself. Will you ruin your honour?

Donkey, look carefully, look, again and again, you can't see my face. You know me, that's why you could recognize me. No one else can realise my body like this. Tell me what to do this time? Answer thoughtfully.

I will marry Jolie. Do whatever you want I won't let go of her hand. If you can cheat on her like this, then listen, I'll be her protector too. I'm with her.

But your honour will be reduced to dust.

Let's go.

At the same time, the honour of our dad won't remain. Think about that too. You can't play such a disgusting game with the respect of our family, Robbie.

I'm not playing, you're doing it.

No. You can't bring such a girl as your wife.

I can bring my wife. And rest assured, I'll do it.

But why?

Because I love her.

And she who loves me, deceived me and agreed to marry you for money? Then?

No. she didn't deceive you. You cheated on her, Robert. Otherwise, why did you make such a video without informing her? Tell me?

Why did she agree to marry you because your income is more than mine? You tell me, first? Answer me?

As far as I know, Jolie, she is not greedy for money. You made a mistake all the time, so she came to me by herself today.

No, I didn't do anything wrong. And you get out of her way.

No. And I will be her. And keep your ears open and listen, if you have auctioned this DVD in the market, I will be a witness against you, and I will tell all the facts to the police. Then let's see, what is jail time? Your father means our father won't be able to save you.

Are you scaring me? You know me well, I have little fear.

I am not afraid, I am ruling you as a younger brother.

So scared of the police?

I'm being forced.

Robert ran out of the house in extreme anger, hatred, and malice.

Robbie didn't go to the store. The shadow came and gave him a cup of tea in the evening, and immediately Jolie's phone rang, "Hello Robbie."

Yes, Jolie.

You weren't told a word.

What are you talking about?

I didn't realise it was a mistake. Could not say the whole thing—predictions of impending weeping.

People make mistakes out of emotion, what's new??

There's something new, Robbie, there's endless sorrow in my forehead.

What's wrong?

Just now, your brother Robert called threatening to auction my character to the market.

And along with that, the intimate moment spent with Robert said everything, including the video. And as soon as she said that, she started crying.

I know. Robert gave me the same threat. However, with one condition, this video will no longer be auctioned off.

What conditions?

If you don't get married, he won't auction this video anymore.

What to do now? My head is not working, my parents will die if they hear this, Robbie.

Robbie let out a huge sigh, "Let's see what can be done? Think about it."

And when you think about it, if he does this defeat in anger?

Wait. Then I will call him first and tell him that I won't marry you.

What? Won't you marry me?

Hey, no, no, if I get married, I'll marry you, Jolie.

Let's find peace. Say, Robbie.

But to handle the situation, I don't mean to take these video clips from him,

Then I will relax and get married.

And if he doesn't give???

I will still marry you, sit back and relax without worrying, and how many days are there for the exam?

One week, I'm going crazy thinking, admit me to the mental hospital now, Robbie. And you're telling me to sit down to read now??

"Yeah. Go and sit down to read." Robbie said in a tone of a proper rule. "And I will take care of this. And yes, we will get married when the exams are over. All the problems will be solved in a month."

Robbie, you're great.

No. I'm not great, I'm ordinary people and men. I don't know what you think of me, but I love you from the heart. So feel free to go. I took responsibility to protect the honour of your family.

I'm so lucky to have you.

Good luck or bad luck to you, time will tell.

Are you giving me oil again?

That is the science learned from you.

I mean, my cat tells me, Mao.

Hmmm

Jolie wanted to dance with joy. When the call cut, Jolie was deeply remorseful for his misdeeds and thought, luckily Robbie had a hand in her life, otherwise what an insult it would have been, and she would have had no choice but to commit suicide.

Bobby entered Robbie's room, "Brother, I have something to tell you."

OK.

Looks like you're too worried? I heard everything Robert said to you from the next room.

Have you heard everything? Then you know what the reason for my concern is.

But I'm also anxious about one thing. Do I a favour?

Say it. Let's see what I can do.

24.

I want to marry Richie, I love her very much.

But Richie is the daughter of our grandmother's sister Miss Nila, so she will be an aunt about us, how is that possible?

We both fell in love. So I don't know anything possible or impossible, and you have to help us with our marriage.

Are you alright? Aunt-nephew love, marriage? No. No, that can't be. Society won't accept, and I won't help you in any work outside these rules. Tell me if you need any other kind of help?

I don't want any other help. Don't say that. I know it's a relationship outside the rules, but does love follow the rules?

Let's see. Let me think first. I'll let you know later. Moreover, I am anxious about one thing now. I will talk about this later.

The next morning, when Robert was on his way to the store, Bobby went to the store and asked for a music movie DVD. And Robert already had a little more devotional love for Bobby. The reason was apparent, though. Bobby was the only one who went to rescue him during the attack on their home that day. As a result, he had to stay in bed for a month. And that day, Robbie fled to save himself. From that day onwards, Robert became vengeful in his mind, and his respect, faith and love for Bobby doubled. And today, when Bobby wanted to stay in his shop on his own, he couldn't ignore it. Instead, he trusted Bobby too much and left him in charge of the shop, wondering if he had a job. However, he didn't say where he was going on.

In the evening, Bobby sat in Robert's shop, and his real purpose was to find a special DVD. The search continued for a long time.

Meanwhile, Robert's courage also increased day by day, and today he went to Jolie's house with four or five others. He raised the DVD issue in front of Jolie's parents and warned her that if they didn't break up Jolie's marriage with Robbie soon, he would openly threaten that the DVD would not take two seconds to auction in the market. Then some more came out of their house with abusive language. Seeing the situation strange, Mrinal Master called Mr Patrick and asked for justice for all the incidents and filth committed by his young son. And if necessary to conduct a police investigation. In his defence, he made it clear that he would fight for his daughter's honour. And until a proper solution is found to this incident, Robbie and Jolie's marriage was postponed.

Today, Jolie's exam, studies have been delayed. Can anyone study after this horrible incident? Even all that has been read so far has vanished from memory. But seeing no way to pass, she wrote a copy of the answer to some critical questions and went to the exam center.

For the first two days, she was very cautious about his coping campaign, hoping that the pass number would come. But on the last day, she was caught for a little distraction and immediately all her treasures were opened. Her paper was a red marked, expelled. Now there was no way but to sit at home and cry.

She is now being punished for a mistake he made unknowingly before. There is also uncertainty about whether she will marry Robbie. And her dream of higher education may be shattered.

People became interested in Mrinal Master, the schoolmaster, and asked him on the street, "What happened?"

He had no answer, so he gave a short answer, "Nothing happened."

Just like that, he had to pass by telling a direct lie. Yet some more curious people don't hesitate to hold him and ask, "If nothing happens, what is Robert saying?"

He may remain silent or angry and annoyed at the answer to this question, saying, "I don't know what Robert is saying."

Robert is talking about your youngest daughter Jolie's character, and you don't know?

Again his short answer was, "No, I don't know."

And without showing the courage to argue from standing, he bowed his head and left to his own house.

Now he doesn't go to the party office in the market every afternoon like before. These are precisely the reasons for the conflict with Mr Patrick. Avoid such unwanted questions only if you are at home. To enter this house after school, and don't go out too much. Go out to buy the only necessities.

Mr Patrick himself blocked the way and forced him to stand. And said, "Wait a minute."

What do you say? What can you say now? Your two sons together ruined my daughter's life and also my honour. I am now forced to hide my face for your youngest son.

I understand everything. So I can't change what has happened. Can't we start anew now?

What do you want to start anew now?

I also see Robbie very depressed day by day, so we give Robbie's marriage to Jolie. Is there any problem?

That's fine - but your youngest son, Robert, has a DVD. So he came to my house with a warning. If Robbie marries Jolie, he will ruin my daughter's honour by publishing it.

I heard about it that day too. Wait. I'll arrange for Robert very soon. I promised you, and you won't go to the police. I beg with folded hands that the baby boy is doing the wrong thing out of emotion. That's why we adults can't throw them in the dark. And besides, he has a future too.

I understand, although he is gossiping about my daughter, it seems that the video has not been shown to anyone yet. When people ask me something in this regard, I avoid.

Then they left with confidence and trust in each other.

On the other hand, as soon as Mithun was released from the hospital, he started following Nisha again. Maintains the continuity of following her, but doesn't go in front of her, doesn't speak annoyingly, only looks at her from a distance.

Even though Nisha sees these things and doesn't bother her like before, she doesn't complain to anyone. And on such a rainy day, when Nisha was returning home from school, she was alone, she didn't have a friend with her that day. None of his friends went to school.

The storm began. Nisha was standing under the mango tree with her bag on her chest and was getting wet. No one is anywhere. Suddenly Mithun appeared in front of him like Jamdut. He handed her an umbrella and said, "Take it, you're getting wet."

I don't need your umbrella. You get out of here now. I have been watching for a long time, you are following me, and if there is any disturbance today, I will be forced to tell everyone.

Why? Are you afraid of me?

Hmmm

Then why did you go to see me with your father in the hospital that day? Answer me.

Your friend Ananta called your parents because you had a big accident, and the doctor said you are fighting for your life. Ananta told your mother that you were repeatedly calling my name 'Nisha, Nisha' before and after your accident. Your parents came to our house with folded hands and begged us to appear to you. I disagreed. Even my parents were furious. But your mother cried a lot when she heard these whims, she said, once you see me, you will get well. So my father took me to the hospital just to keep your parent's mind. Nothing else, now you're well, you're following me again, but it's not right.

So you went to the hospital at my mother's request?

Yes, And Ananta knows everything. Ananta had talked to the doctor and told us the same thing on the phone. You had a significant injury in your brain, you could go into a coma, so we were forced to go to the hospital that day to save your life. You are well now. And don't disturb me in any way. I'm afraid of you because you're a bad boy. Stay away from me.

Mithun couldn't answer this anymore, the storm stopped for a while, and Nisha also finished talking and started walking.

Mithun was standing alone on the floor of that famous mango tree. His body was soaking wet in the rainwater. For a long time, he had abstained from alcohol and prostitution for which, she feared and didn't love him. But it is difficult to prove that he has become good because of past misdeeds. Nisha told the truth, "You're so bad." The same words "You're so bad, I'm afraid of you," kept ringing in his ears. Who knows how long it took? Suddenly the phone rang,

Hello, Mithun.

Yes, what happened?

The police stopped me at the Teesta Bridge. Arrested and detained your car. I am at the police station now. Bail me if you can.

Mithun understood that it was meant to be, sin is never suppressed.

The two of them used to carry sacks, but they would get the original rent four times to move the goods. The owner who took the goods in their car had strict instructions not to touch it until the goods reached the specified address. Out of curiosity, the packet was sealed to be a clear proof as soon as anyone opened it. So the two of them didn't show so much courage, what is inside the bag? There were illegal weapons, marijuana and heroin.

But the owner of the goods denied everything and went into hiding.

For the first time in his life, a rising leftist youth leader, Jeet Roy, appeared at the house of Congress leader Mr Oni. Again alone. Despite having many servants, Mr Oni's wife Neelima made tea for Jeet by herself, even though it was according to her husband's instructions.

Mr Oni said, "Why did the sun suddenly rise in the west today, Jeet?"

No, the sun still rises in the east. Can't I come to your house?

No, I didn't say that. Tell me, why did you come here with so much trouble?

Bobby and Richie's love story began anew. They met again as before and talked on the phone. Both are passionate lovers of the sea of youth, but the society became a massive obstacle behind their marriage and attaining perfection. That's why now they both argued that if Ravi-Jolie gets married first, they will get married with their help even if it is with the consent of the parents. So Bobby is trying hard to get this marriage, but this path became a thorn in the side of Robert's blueprint DVD. Now stop working. Bobby is looking for a DVD day and night. All the evidence will be smashed if found, and there will be no obstacle in Robbie's marriage.

Robert usually returns home late at night, and their two brothers have the same bedroom, although the beds are separate, all searches are over, and now this bedroom is left, but even if he hides in so many things in such a big room, where did he keep it? It won't take less than a day. So that night Bobby decided in his mind that when Robert went to his shop tomorrow morning, Robbie and he would look for this DVD together in this room if necessary. For the time being, Bobby fell asleep after a little talk with Richie about this decision.

There are giant banyan trees in the distance, there is no neon light on the side of the road, and no one can see anyone's face.

What I wore in the case, I was terrified. Do you know? I didn't think the case would end so soon and I would get bail. We were deceived. We didn't know there was a gun inside the bag. Did you know?

No, what would I take if I knew? And we also have faults. Why didn't I understand that I was tempted to get four times more rent? That's why

You told Sudhir Das, today's incident?

I said on the phone, he refused. Later I went to his house, and his wife said he was not at home. Where did he go, didn't say anything? He didn't say when he would come.

Then say? Why did the police release me, at first they slapped me a lot, then they did nothing and released me.

Then I went to Mr Patrick to save you from the case. I cried a lot holding her feet. Sudhir Das had a gun inside his bag. I said everything. He then called someone from the district leadership and went to the next room, then called and said they had released you. And he took my phone number. And he said he would call later.

Great.

There seems to be a mystery.

We very ordinary people don't understand so much deception. It is a matter of those leaders and ministers. And I sat in jail today for the sin of greed for more than two hundred rupees under the pressure of lack of family. I was lucky, so I survived.

Will I get the car back? What do you think? Or will you have to lose the vehicle for such a profit? Being worried.

When Mr Patrick can save me, I think you can keep your car. And we don't know anything about it. Sudhir Das is Mr Oni's special man. Did he use to smuggle illegal goods in these sacks?

I don't understand. It may be that Mr Oni has no secret affair with Sudhir in this matter. Sudhir Das has a connection with any high-level smuggler without informing him.

Maybe, nothing is impossible. Let's go home now. As soon as Ananta left, Mr Patrick's call came to Mithun's phone.

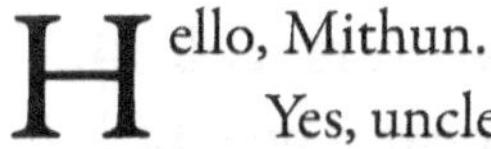

25.

Hello, Mithun.

Yes, uncle.

You will meet me tomorrow. I have something to say to you.

Well uncle, but when will I come?

Come this evening, I'll be home.

All right. But Uncle, I'm innocent. Believe me, I don't know anything about this. My car is stuck in the police station, will I get it back? If not, it will be defeated.

See what I can do, try to get back. But come tomorrow. Then we will talk.

After these short words, the line was cut, from two sides.

Early in the sunrise, the shadow at Mr Patrick's house went to work with his waist tied early in the morning. People in the whole place started chirping as soon as it was morning.

Neomi understands very well that Rakesh has been following her for a long time, but she has no idea about Rakesh's personal life. So this morning, when Bobby went to the betel garden to brush his teeth. Then Neomi was cleaning the back of the house.

Bobby?

Yes, what happened?

What kind of person is Rakesh?

Why? Has he mistreated you?

"No, he didn't. But it's a good idea to know a little bit. That's it," she said, clenching her teeth.

So, what do you want to know about him?

That he got married, didn't he? That's it.

I heard that he has a wife and children in Bihar, but I have not seen him go home even once in these five years. Is there anyone at all, who knows?

Well, got it. All right. I will do a lot of work now.

Yes, go.

In Neomi's mind, there were only different things about Rakesh, a lot. Nothing is clear, yet why her mind became restless. Not bad looking, tall wide, but a little black. I am not getting married either, every proposal that comes to see me, all marriages are breaking up. I have come to this aunt's house, and now I can eat three meals a day, I am getting the right dress. These were dreams one day. After a long time, I saw the happy face of getting a little stuff.

In the middle of the dishes washing, Neomi began to speak to itself. That's why her hand broke a cup. So her mood is terrible. No matter how bad the mood is, is there anything called mood for poor? However, you have to die after serving. So she went to water the flower garden and saw who had already given water. Great! Who gave? Just don't understand. So, she went to clean the rooms. At first, she went to Bobby's room. The door slammed shut from the inside. She knocked on the door. Bobby opens the door, "What happened?"

Nothing happened. I will clean the room.

No, you don't have to clean this room today.

Why?

Cleaning my room is complete.

All right. Are you doing anything by closing the door?

Yes, working. (Searching for the DVD.) Now you go.

Well,

Where did the sunrise? Not having to do any work. I see Robbie's room. No, there is no one here. If caught cheating too much, it will be a scandal. So I have to clean all the rooms like a polite girl. Rakesh said from behind, "Neomi?"

Yes,

Can I help you clean the room?

Did I say that?

No, I heard you have back pain?

OK. Just clean this room.

At noon Arupa and Nayan came to Mr Patrick.

The two of them sat on the floor of her room, Bobby, turned on the T.V. Rakesh is doing her job, so Neomi watched T.V. with Arupa and Nayan. But Mr Patrick told Neomi to get out of the room, there is an urgent matter with Nayan and Arupa which he is reluctant to say in front of him.

Then Neomi necessarily left the room and went back to work.

Mr Patrick assigned the two of them to look after Sudhir Das, a few days ago, that day they took their claim to him in person. Sudhir Das's house was next to the two of them because the hero of the gun attack on Jeet has not been caught yet. Since Sudhir Das's name was on the list of suspects, these two detectives were put on them, because Sudhir Das's house was next to their home, so the job was easy for them.

Meanwhile, Mr Patrick thought that a gun was found in the bag sent by Sudhir Das in Mithun's car. So he called Mithun again in the evening. Now somehow this Sudhir Das has confirmed the victory. Thinking about all this, the two of them, namely Arupa and Nayan, came. According to the report received from them, secret meetings are held at Sudhir Das's house every night, outsiders also come by bike, what is discussed is whispered. Even if you eavesdrop on the fence, you can't hear it.

At the same time, on the other hand, Bobby and Robbie closed the room and were looking for that DVD since morning. The cupboards, the beds, the floor of the bed, the showcase, the books on the table, the clothes were all turned upside down, but after so much hard work, when it was not found. At that time, in extreme despair, both of them were seeing the darkness in their eyes, thinking that they would have to tidy them again, so both of them were relaxing with the responsibility of tidying up the house.

Robert entered the house from the store at noon. He took rest after lunch at noon. Then goes to the store again in the afternoon. Even today, the opposite has not happened. But as soon as he entered the house today, he was called to Mr Patrick's room, and Neomi informed Robert.

Robert is present in front of his dad.

What happened?

Yes, I have something to say to you.

Robert leaned back on the sofa.

I heard you have a DVD, a dirty video of Jolie. Did you make it?

Yes.

You give me all that.

But why?

I'll ruin them, and marry Robbie to Jolie. That's my decision.

I won't give them, and I don't want to see Jolie as Robbie's wife in this house.

This is my last word in this house, you may be forgetting.

No, I haven't forgotten, but that can't be given.

Then I will be forced to hand you over to the police.

Whatever you please, I won't give.

Is this your last word!

Yes.

Mr Patrick immediately called the police in front of him and told the law all the facts. Meanwhile, Robbie and Bobby Come on, they also ask Robert a lot, to give him the DVD but in the end to no avail.

Eventually, the police arrived, and Robert was taken away and told when leaving, "we know how to open the mouth in these cases."

In the evening Mithun came to see him again, he got many reports about Sudhir Das from Mithun.

The news of Robert's arrest at his father's hands soon became known throughout the village, and he was widely praised as a leader and a father. On hearing this, Mrinal Master also expressed his sorrow, came home and consoled Mr Patrick.

Jeet came in the night, Mr Patrick discussed various issues with him.

Mr Patrick was devastated by multiple tensions, but he always covered his weakness.

Suddenly Mr Patrick got excited, he arranged the marriage of Robbie and Jolie. And the wedding took place fifteen days later. And Robert will be then in jail.

Meanwhile, Jeet appeared with good news, just a week before the wedding. Finally, Robert opened his mouth. But the DVD is no longer in his hands. Whoever has it, he is a relative of Sudhir Das, but Mr Oni doesn't know any of this.

Sudhir managed to do what Mr Oni could not do even after becoming the local Congress leader. Now Sudhir was running his illegal business by deceiving everyone.

But Jeet became a thorn in the way. Jeet had secretly consulted with Mr Patrick that day and called the police. So Mithun's car was caught selectively, and that suspicion was proved. So Sudhir Das left his house in this village in just ten days and went to the city with his wife and child. Immediately all relations with Mr Oni were severed. Because Mithun went to Mr Oni. After revealing all the facts to him, Mr Oni frankly admitted that Sudhir Das was the mastermind behind the mass uprising at Mr Patrick's house before the election.

So despite being a member of the same group, Sudhir Das's path became different. Because humanity is before Mr Oni, the team is much later. And that is why even though there was a factional dispute with Jeet and Mr Patrick, the ally began to behave thoughtfully.

The essence of Jeet's meeting with Mr Oni that day was a secret meeting of Jeet's land and Anil's land in one line. So there will be a vast tea garden on the land of the two of them, and Mr Patrick will build a factory on his land. So even though the three of them are now different parties, they have become one for the sake of their income. Just in these few days. How many people change colours for their interests, who knows? And it is possible, because of the dishonesty of this Sudhir Das, so Mr Oni agreed to this proposal.

26.

Two years have passed.

Jolie was married to Robbie and was living a happy married life. Jolie failed the exam but passed the next time.

Robert returned from prison for his father, but the DVD was never recovered. So even though Jolie is Robbie's wife, the DVD mystery is not over yet.

The protagonist of all the events denied all about the DVD, and Robert also became a fool. Sudhir Das was imprisoned for a few days, but due to the prominent leaders' recommendation and lack of evidence, it has not been possible for anyone to arrest Sudhir Das yet. Now he walks behind the principal leaders of the City.

On the other hand, in these two years, Mithun and Ananta are now close to Mr Patrick. But even today, the attacker of Jeet was not caught that night. Mithun is now leaving the muddy path like before, trying to get better but Nisha still doesn't trust him.

Ravi Jolie's marriage also took place. Kalpana and Mr Patrick went to Ananta's house and invited them. They all forgot Lesa's grief in marriage, and everyone loved Robbie very much, so Anjana herself blessed Robbie with her hands on his head.

Meanwhile, Bobby and Richie are not married, they still love each other as before. How long will this continue? They both wanted to get close to each other, but no one favoured their marriage. Not a single person. They are still very helpless. Bobby hasn't had a relationship with Neha in the last two years, which has deepened his love for Richie. So they decided to escape away from home.

Richie and Bobby made all sorts of plans to escape from the house. In the morning just before the escape, Richie packed up four large bags. Meanwhile, Nila came forward and asked the reason for this arrangement, Richie had not told anyone before. Nila's very natural and curious question is, "Why are you packing so many bags? Shall you going somewhere or not?"

I would say today. Tomorrow I am going to a friend's house in Siliguri. I am currently on leave. Then we will go for a walk together.

Who else is going?

Few more will go. You have no reason to worry so much about it?

That's right. But you told your father?

No, not yet. You tell me

Well.

Richie told his mother all these lies, keeping secret that she had planned to escape away with Bobby. If her father and elder brother find out, she will be locked in a room. Thinking about all this, he sat in silence.

"What are you thinking so much in silence?" Nila said,

I am going out for the first time in life. So there is a tension.

Everything will be fine. Don't worry anymore—a matter of a few days. When you come back, we will all go for a walk together. All right??

"What else will you see in this life? Your unfaithful daughter is a big loser, a criminal," Richie said to herself.

And at the same time, Bobby entered his sister-in-law, Jolie's room, "Jolie, may I come?"

Yes, come on.

From the beginning, Jolie loves Bobby as her brother. There is a massive reason behind this. Ever since she came to this house, Robert has never spoken to her, respecting is so far. Because very simple, Robert's old enmity with Jolie. In that case, Bobby is always an exception and has always appreciated Jolie like an elder sister, so Jolie loves Bobby like her own brother.

Now Bobby enters Jolie's room, pulling the curtain first. Jolie asked curiously, "Which secret will tell you something?"

"Yeah, very, very secretive, no one can be told except you." He came and sat in the front chair. Jolie got out of bed, pulled up another chair, and sat down in front of him. Jolie said, "Say it now. Looks like there's no one around. Neomi in the kitchen now. Robbie, Robert, your dad won't come home before 2 PM."

Bobby began to say in a shallow voice, "I love Richie very much. You know what?"

Yes, I know everything. You continue.

But no one will accept our marriage. We are not so lucky. No one will arrange anything for us. Nothing will happen in our marriage as we did at your wedding. None of our hopes will be fulfilled.

Somewhere in Jolie's mind, there was a deep pain for Bobby. But these words are actual forever. There is no way to argue. There was no way to comfort him in vain, only heartache.

Bobby began to say again, "I told Robbie many times to help us before your marriage, but he didn't. Although that's normal." Bobby let out a huge sigh. The painful last sound of this sigh pierced Jolie's heart like an arrow.

Jolie began to say, "I'm by your side. How can I help you?"

"It's too big. At least you stood by me," Bobby's eyes twinkled with joy. He kept saying, "How much more can you do alone? That is what you said. We are running away tomorrow. People will say that Bobby Chowdhury, f Mr Patrick Chowdhury's son, ran away and married his aunt. What a shame!"

Say, yet you flee. If you stay here, no one will ever understand your love. What to do? I don't see any other way but to escape away. But your father should not know in any way.

Dad, no one knows why. You just found out. Don't tell anyone.

Rest assured, I won't tell your brother this either. Where are you going?

For now, we will go to Siliguri, I will rent a house. Now Richie has taken a 15-day leave saying that Richie can go around. When the holiday is over, we will come back from Siliguri, I will bring her to the office.

Okay, it will take much less time to get to Siliguri by bike than by bus. That would be good.

Bobby was crying profusely, and Jolie's eyes filled with tears. The boy who has been cherished as the only brother in life, who has respected and honoured her, will escape away tomorrow but she has nothing to do. She started thinking to herself again, "What duty could she do for the brother who has cherished for so long? Alas, the heart of a woman. «

Jolie kept thinking that after coming to this father-in-law's house, she could only think of Bobby as her own except Robbie.

I bless you, you will be happy. God will give you a wonderful son.

"So be it," he said and tried to smile with tears in his eyes.

Jolie said, "You can go when you go, and I won't stop you. But if there's a problem, if you need money, feel free to call, go with the account number. Don't forget that your sister is still alive."

Yes, I will. I will say without hesitation. I knew you wouldn't disappoint me. And I will be after everyone, I will never be able to come in front of my father in my life. Dad will abandon me, I will never be able to go in front of mom again, and I will never be able to call her 'mom'. Love is so criminal. "

Yes, love is very criminal.

At that moment, Robbie entered the room, and Bobby was about to wipe away his tears. Robbie asked him, "What happened Bobby? Why are you crying?"

"No, nothing happened," said Bobby.

Ravi looked at Jolie and saw that she was also crying. What do you mean, I know?

Robbie said in his mind, "What happened? Why is everyone crying? No one said anything."

Bobby was packing his bags in the afternoon, and then Mr Patrick entered his room.

27.

Bobby, are you in the room?

Yes, Dad, I am.

Mr Patrick removed the curtain and entered the room. Mr Patrick sat down in the corner of the bed, shaking his legs and said, "So many bags? Shall you go somewhere or not?"

Hmm, I am going on a tour with college friends.

When to go?

Tomorrow,

Did you tell mom? And what about your business?

Not yet. But I will say at night, and I am doing business well. Ten lakh rupees profit was made this month, you have not been paid yet, I will pay later.

Bobby thought to himself, not a single penny of this month's profit can be given to you. I have to do new business with money. So I won't hesitate to resort to lies.

Seeing the boy's silence, Mr Patrick said, "Take care of the business. Stop being childish."

Yes, Dad.

And what about Rakesh. He has an excellent relationship with Sudhir Das.

Is that so? Where? Didn't Rakesh tell me anything?

What will Rakesh himself say? Do you keep his information? Sudhir Das is a dangerous man, so I have serious suspicions. From now on, to bring raw materials and supply things, you will never leave him alone and go with him. It's my order.

"Yeah, Dad," Bobby lied again.

After saying this, Mr Patrick asked again, "When will you be back?"

After four or five days.

Okay, the truck won't be out in these days. I'll permit to get the car out when you get back. And where are you going? I want the address, and I also like the phone numbers of those going with you.

Yeah,

When you are leaving?

Tomorrow at seven o'clock we will all meet in Siliguri, and then we will decide where we are going.

Okay.

All right, Dad.

"One more thing, you're still in a relationship with Richie. I keep track of everyone. I have a spy everywhere. Stop it, Bobby. Don't ruin my dignity. I don't like this filth at all. I've told you many times before." I still saying. "Saying this, he went to his room.

In the evening Robbie went to meet Bobby. In the meantime, Neomi went to the two brothers with tea. Robbie "What happened to you? Why are you lying down?"

No, nothing happened. Why all of a sudden in my room?

No, just like that. I will talk to you today.

With me?

Hmmm. What happened to you? I can see a massive change in you.

You're thinking the opposite.

Well, then you tell me the truth.

Which truth?

Why did you come out of Jolie's room crying at noon? Why are you so sad?

"Where? I didn't cry. You saw something wrong," he said, sipping a cup of tea.

Robbie sipped his tea and said, "I either didn't see it wrong, but now you're sitting in front of my eyes. Your eyes are still swollen. Is it wrong for me to see?"

My body is not well. So it seems. I'm fine now. I'm going on a tour tomorrow, with college friends.

Good. But I will ask a question, will you answer exactly? I love you so much as a brother, you know it very well, so if you have a little faith or love in me, you will give the right answer to my question today.

Yes, tell me?

Are you escaping away with Richie?

Bobby fell from the sky like a spark of lightning. Didn't Jolie say that? Neither Jolie can do that. Again, he could not lie after losing to his brother's unconditional love. Bobby quietly lowered his neck and sat in front of his brother, trying to hide his face as much as possible.

Is this Bobby? Why are you crying?

Robbie's tea is over. So he got up from the chair, put a hand on his brother's back and turned gently. He said, "Don't cry so much. You think Jolie has told me everything. No, Jolie didn't tell me anything. I guess I said. Why you are crying again? I caught you."

This time Bobby succumbed to emotion and told Robbie, "Yes, I'm escaping away with Richie."

28.

I know you're going to do this.

"Yeah, that's what I'm doing. Forgive me. Please, don't tell anyone." Bobby said, sobbing.

Robbie, like these children of his brother, gave in to the heartbreaking cries and said, "Well, that's fine. I won't tell anyone. Stop crying. Why have you been crying like a child since then? And you can rest assured I won't tell anyone. Listen, call me. I'll help you in any way I can. "

Yes, I'll call. You know, I feel very, very helpless. Dad told me today that I would be unhappy if I didn't leave Richie. Dad cursed me. Well, the curse of the parents becomes true, Isn't it?

Robbie was not mentally prepared for such a difficult situation. Now he can no longer handle the situation.

Still, Robbie kept saying, "Brother, don't cry anymore. Everyone will listen. Calm down a little. Everything will be fine. I am here."

"No, nothing will be fine," Bobby began to cry again. Robbie got up and closed the door so that the sound of crying in the room would not go out.

Just as Robbie is comforting his brother, on that poisonous evening night, another detached bird, soaked in this sea of love, is lying on the edge of the bed, thinking about his demise. She refuses to cry today. She can't call today. Crying can be caught. Still, Richie's heart was pounding with tears. Richie pressed another stone on his chest. Even though she died of a heart attack, she is not allowed to cry today. Because in this poor man's home there is no separate room to mourn.

The much-anticipated morning came, another new sun rose in the eastern sky, another recent history began.

Ignoring everyone, Bobby left the house. Rakesh has been told to leave his bike at a specific place in the City. But Rakesh has not said anything about his plan to escape away with Richie. Bobby told Nimai last night to come to the town with Richie, and he came to City in a truck with Rakesh. After saying goodbye to Rakesh, he took his bike and went to a friend Ajit's house. The bike will stay at Ajit's home for now. From there Bobby met Richie. Then he got in Nimai's car and sat down. The car was speeding towards Siliguri. Two animals were sitting in the City in fear.

Nimai's car stopped at the Siliguri Airview intersection, "This is my last stop, Bobby."

Yes, that's right. Stop right here.

Shall I say something?

Tell me?

Will you go to marry Richie and that's why you are escaping?

Yes, I came. You won't tell anyone.

Well, I won't say. Be happy.

"Nimai Please don't tell anyone. Otherwise, we will fall in difficulty" Richie said.

Richie, you are safe. You know I won't betray.

Nimai left.

Richie asked Bobby, "What are you going to do now, Bobby? Where are we going?"

We move to Calcutta. It would not be right for us to be around here.

Yes, you are right. Then your father will find us.

Now no train tickets will be available. And flight tickets won't be available, I told my father that I am going to Kolkata on a flight tomorrow, so I can't go around the airport.

Yes, I also said I would go to Darjeeling, so I won't go there either.

Come on, the bus just for us.

The two of them left for the bus stand in an auto.

In the morning, the son of the house next to Richie, Paltu, the deceased Emma's brother, was standing and brushing his teeth, when he saw Richie getting into Nimai's car with so many bags. He came home and asked his mother, "Where is Richie going?"

How do I know?

Later, however, the matter was forgotten.

In the afternoon, while sitting in the Robert shop in the market, he talked about getting into Richie's car in the morning.

Robert closes the shop. He left for home and thought to himself, "this morning I saw Bobby going somewhere with a bag. And when he left, he said he was going to visit Calcutta with his friends. Once I should call Bobby."

Hello.

Yes, Robert. What happened?

Where are you now?

Why? I am in Siliguri, at the airport. I told you everything yesterday.

And Richie is with you?

Why? What are you talking about? Why will she stay with me? She is in their house.

No, she's not home. She drove in Nimai's car in the morning. Paltu saw it with his own eyes.

I don't know where she goes.

You are lying. Tell the truth. Otherwise, I will be forced to tell these things to dad.

"Do whatever you want. I don't have Richie with me."

Robert called Bobby several times on his way home from the market but constantly heard busy. He was burning with anger.

Robert came home and went straight to Mr Patrick's room.

On the other hand, standing next to Bobby, Richie overheard Robert talking to Bobby. Frightened, Bobby's hand tightened, and she began to tremble. And asked, "What did Robert say?"

Nothing. Don't worry.

Richie said, "I'm scared. What if I get caught? What happens? Do you think anything?"

No, we won't be caught in any way. Nothing else will happen to you. I am with you. Don't worry. And it can't be too late. You sit here and guard the luggage; I'll get the ticket by then.

Well. Come on, I'm scared.

Nothing will happen to us. I'm with you. What are you afraid of?

Your father and my elder brother are both like Hitler. If we got caught in their hands at this moment, they would kill us, will burn alive.

I said nothing will happen. You sit quietly. I will go and come.

When Bobby went to the ticket counter and bought two AC sleeper tickets for the Kolkata-bound bus, Robbie's phone rang, "Hello, Bobby?"

Yes, something happened?

You don't go on a flight, you don't go on a train,

We are not going on any flight or train. We are going by bus.

All right, keep it up, now.

Robbie stood outside Mr Patrick's room and heard Robert tell his father all about Bobby and Richie's escape. So he quickly called Bobby again, "Hello, Bobby?"

Yes, any news?

No, now is not the time to say anything. Dad can call you directly. You won't receive it. Switch off the phone. Just now.

Why? Is something wrong?

Nothing happened. Now is not the time to talk so much, when is your car?

This will leave in fifteen minutes. Well, well done. But later I will call and tell me where you went. And switch off the phone now, soon.

Yes, I do.

Both of them cut the line.

Mr Patrick, holding a firecracker, first called Jeet and told him about it.

Jeet said, "They seem to have escape away on their own. Where to look now?"

You now search all the stands in Siliguri with the people. The railway station, airport, bus stand, everywhere.

When did they go out, uncle?

In the morning.

So they are sitting in Siliguri so far? I don't think so.

Then tell the police?

No, there will be no profit. They are both adults. I don't think there will be any benefit in telling the police. The law will speak for them, and your reputation will be ruined by the public outcry.

That's right. So, as a father, I will sit and watch the scene? You find another way soon. If necessary, take the help of the police. I call Bobby right now.

But Bobby just turned off his phone as per Robbie's instructions. So he couldn't talk to Bobby even after trying many times. He sat for a while in frustration. Suddenly it seems that Richie has a phone. So he called Richie's father Avinash and told him everything. And asked to talk to his daughter.

Avinash heard this from Mr Patrick and insulted Richie's mother for a while. Then he called Richie.

Richie, on the other hand, received the call, "Hello Dad. Tell me."

29.

"Where are you now?" Avinash asked Richie angrily.

Why? I'm at my friend's house now.

Well, a good thing, where is your friend's house in Siliguri? Give me the address? Right now.

Why? What happened?

Nothing happened. There is a need. I asked you to give the address.

What to do with the address?

I said I need it. I will come.

What will you do when you come? We are no longer there now. We're out.

"Don't get a place to be rude. Rude girl, have you started a Drama? You escape away with Bobby by cheating on us, and now you're making up a lie?" Impossibly angry, he said the words threateningly.

After hearing all the truth from his father, Richie couldn't answer, so she kept quiet.

Avinash continued, "I am telling Francis right now. He will cut you into pieces and feed the fox and the dog. Honour.........

Richie cut off the call before it was over. Richie is disappointed to see Bobby leave his luggage behind. Bobby said, "What happened to you?"

Dad called. Everyone knows everything.

I know. Everyone will call again.

Meanwhile, the car was also starting. For the first time in her life, Richie got into such a long-distance vehicle.

Meanwhile, Mr Patrick came out of the room and started cursing Kalpana Devi. Kalpana cried when she heard all this. Jolie ran to Kalpana's room and said, "What happened, mom? Why are you crying?" Jolie came and sat next to Kalpana.

Kalpana cried and narrated the whole incident to Jolie.

Jolie, knowing everything in advance, reassured him, "Mom, what's the use of crying now? You'll get sick if you cry too much."

Richie and Bobby are now sitting side by side in this small chip. Richie said, "I'm having a severe headache, Bobby? I think I'll vomit all over your body."

If you do. So what happened? You are my wife, and so be out of tension. Put your head on my chest and fall asleep. You haven't eaten since morning. Now take a nap. If the body feels healthy, we will sit here and eat together. "

No, I won't sleep. I can't sleep at all today. There is so much joy in so much hardship. You know how many days my dream has come true. Tell me? I cried for you for so many days and nights, so today I found you my own. We will have a happy family. You and I will have a cute child who will call you dad and call me mom. How long have I dreamed for about all this, you know, Bobby?

Hmmm, I know.

If you know, give me a kiss now.

I will kiss you for a thousand hours. Now you are definitely mine.

That's how Bobby and Richie crossed over to the unknown. To make their love come true. To make each other your own.

It was late at night, and the two of them landed at Bahrampur in Murshidabad and went up to Hotel Rudra, a hotel known to Bobby. He told everyone about Calcutta, so they went down without going to Calcutta. The two of them came to the room, turned on the AC, lay down on a bed, under a blanket, and fell into a deep sleep. Now the two statues are homeless beyond the reach of the known boundaries.

It's morning. The police started searching, but their whereabouts were not found. So, the police tried to persuade Mr Patrick to accept everything since they were adults. But Mr Patrick kept his promise. He tried hard but could not communicate with Bobby. Because the day after that incident, Bobby broke his and Richie's phone.

Don't miss out!

Visit the website below and you can sign up to receive emails whenever Sundari Gibran publishes a new book. There's no charge and no obligation.

https://books2read.com/r/B-A-IPDO-VDGNC

BOOKS2READ

Connecting independent readers to independent writers.

Also by Sundari Gibran

Pranayama: The Yoga Breath
Characterless